WHO SHE WAS

MARTINA MONROE BOOK 9

H.K. CHRISTIE

ALSO BY H.K. CHRISTIE

The Martina Monroe Series —a nail-biting crime thriller series starring PI Martina Monroe and her unofficial partner Detective August Hirsch of the Cold Case Squad. If you like high-stakes games, jaw-dropping twists, and suspense that will keep you on the edge of your seat, then you'll love the Martina Monroe crime thriller series.

The Selena Bailey Series (1 - 5) — a suspenseful series featuring a young Selena Bailey and her turbulent path to becoming a top-notch private investigator as led by her mentor, Martina Monroe.

The Val Costa Series —a gripping crime thriller with heart-pounding suspense. If you love Martina, you'll love Val.

The Neighbor Two Doors Down —a dark and witty psychological thriller. If you like unpredictable twists, page-turning suspense, and unreliable narrators, then you'll love *The Neighbor Two Doors Down*.

A Permanent Mark A heartless killer. Weeks without answers. Can she move on when a murderer walks free? If you like riveting suspense and gripping mysteries then you'll love *A Permanent Mark* - starring a grown up Selena Bailey.

For H.K. Christie's full catalog go to: **www.authorhkchristie.com**

At **www.authorhkchristie.com** you can also sign up for the H.K. Christie reader club where you'll be the first to hear about upcoming novels, new releases, giveaways, promotions, and a free e-copy of the prequel to the Martina Monroe Thriller Series, *Crashing Down*!

Cover design by Odile Stamanne

www.authorhkchristie.com

First edition: June 2023

ISBN: 978-1-953268-16-7

012225h

For the survivors

1

———

FERN

IN A FOG OF DESPERATION, I dragged her lifeless body over to the pit. It was heavier than expected, and I had to use every muscle in my body to shove her into the hole. With the resulting thud, I was irrevocably changed.

Shovel in hand, I set out to finish the job. The sound of dirt hitting her body echoed like firecrackers in my mind. What seemed like hours later, I paused and stared at her grave. Dark thoughts swirled, and I used all my mental strength to shake them and continue on. Complete the task. My hands continued to tremble as I scooped up the last pile of soil and dumped it onto the dark mound. Sweat soaked my shirt, and my back ached. My soul felt tarnished.

I remembered my childhood and the small, simple dreams I'd once had. How innocently I begged my parents for a kitten or a puppy, only to be rebuffed time and time again. Dad was allergic, and Dad was in charge. He wouldn't budge, no matter how much I pleaded.

It was why I'd left home—to forge my own path, away from the constraints of his rules. But standing over a pile of freshly dug earth containing something far more sinister, I had to wonder how things had gotten this far.

I wiped my brow, feeling the weight of my actions settling in my chest. The man I loved had led me down a dark path, one I couldn't escape from easily. He'd asked me to do things I never knew I was capable of, things that had damaged me beyond repair.

Why had I gone along with it?

Was I so blinded by love I didn't see what was really happening until it was too late? I wondered if the man I'd fallen for was not the person I thought he was. Was he everything I left home to escape?

My body trembled as the realization hit me. All signs pointed to yes.

He had a darkness in him I couldn't understand. But it wasn't until he handed me a gun and instructed me to pull the trigger that I realized how far I'd strayed from my own moral code.

As I stood there, staring at the grave I'd just filled, the sun poked through the treetops and placed a spotlight on the dirt. I took a deep breath and looked up at the sky. Looking for what? A sign? A sense that the events of the last two hours weren't real? Could I get past this? Could I go on as if I was unmoved?

He approached. "Looks like you're about done."

"Just finished."

"Nice. What are you thinking about?" he asked, stepping closer.

I backed away, feeling the hairs on the back of my neck stand up. "Nothing." My voice was barely above a whisper.

He reached out to touch my arm. "It takes a little getting used to. But you and I both know you had to do it. She threatened our way of life."

His eyes met mine, and I knew I had to pretend to be okay.

I forced a smile, willing my hands to stop shaking. "Yeah," I said, my voice steady. "I guess we did what we had to do."

His face held a Cheshire grin. "Good. I'm glad you understand."

But I didn't understand, not really. My mind was still reeling from what had just happened. I'd killed someone. Buried them in the ground like a piece of garbage. How could I possibly be okay with that?

As he turned to walk away, I took a deep breath and forced my body to appear calm. I had to play the part, act like everything was normal. If he suspected anything was off, he might hurt me, too.

As we walked away from the site of my crime, I couldn't help but ponder what had led me there. I couldn't blame everything on him, even though he had guided me on a journey I never thought possible. I had made the choice to stay with him, to trust him blindly, and to follow his lead.

But now, as I looked at him beside me, I saw his true colors. He was a monster, a shell of a man who had no regard for human life. And I was stuck with him, trapped in his world. I couldn't help but feel a sense of dread wash over me. How long would it be until he turned on me? How long until I was the one six feet under, buried in this imitation utopia?

But then again, maybe it was better that way. If I were dead, I wouldn't have to live with the guilt and shame of what I had done. Maybe death was the only escape from the nightmare I was living in.

2

———

MARTINA

Storming in with a piping-hot cup of coffee, I flashed a warm smile at Mrs. Pearson and stopped to glance above her desk, where the company name was proudly displayed: Drakos Monroe Security & Investigations. When I'd first joined this business, I never dreamed my name would be on the company stationery. I found myself longing for Jared to witness what I had accomplished. Would he have believed it? If I were honest, I could barely believe it was true myself. It would have been nice to share this triumph with him. After all, Monroe was his name.

Eight years had passed since Jared's death, and yet, I thought of him every single day. Perhaps it was because I was working at the company we once shared, or maybe it was because I saw a reflection of his beautiful blue eyes in Zoey's every day.

So much had changed since I'd lost Jared. His absence had led to a period of losing myself. However, the concept of a time with Jared, not being a single parent or not having a teenager, seemed foreign. There were countless aspects of my life I took immense pride in, accomplishments I had never envisioned for myself. Among these was a milestone I held dear: I was eight years sober, with a token in my back pocket to prove it. Attending meetings had become as routine as hitting the gym, both forming integral parts of my daily life.

But today was special.

Today marked a shift.

I had finally decided I was ready, and I had the energy and the time to give back and become a sponsor.

Eight years ago, deep at the bottom of the abyss, my sponsor, Rocco, held my hand as I took each step to climb back into the light.

I had resisted taking on such an enormous responsibility. Being a single mother, a private investigator, and a business owner all at once was daunting. But my social life was minimal, mostly consisting of time spent with my closest friends, and Zoey, my daughter, seemed to need me less and less. Despite my initial resistance, I had to admit I had the time.

"How was your meeting, dear?" Mrs. Pearson asked.

"It was fantastic. I met my sponsee today."

"That's wonderful," Mrs. Pearson responded, her voice filled with joy. "I've always admired you so much, Martina. All you've been through. All the challenges you've endured. I think you're an incredible individual."

I tried not to laugh. Mrs. Pearson was a force to be reckoned with. She appeared to be a grandmotherly woman who loved her magenta lipstick and sitting behind the reception desk, greeting everyone like they were family. One might assume she was retired, her children out of the house, and that was why she took the job. But no, Mrs. Pearson had been with the company since the very beginning, when Stavros opened the doors. Nothing slipped past her. She was the linchpin of the entire organization. She had heart and strength. I hoped that when I was her age, I would still have that kind of fight inside of me.

"I appreciate that," I responded. "I suppose it takes one to know one."

"I suppose it does. Vincent asked me to tell you he's in his cubicle, and he's ready."

Was Vincent ever not ready? *Oh, to be young again.* "Great. Thanks."

"You take care."

"You too." I sauntered over to Vincent's cubicle, where he was intently staring at the screen, tapping furiously on the keyboard. "Hey, Vincent. Mrs. Pearson says you're ready."

"That I am, Martina. They should be here in a few minutes."

Working with Vincent made it seem like the days at the CoCo County Sheriff's Department weren't so long ago. In reality, it had been over five years. Sometimes I missed those times, but working with Stavros and the team brought me a lot of satisfaction. It gave me the time to be there for Zoey. I was her only parent, and when her grandmother moved in with Sarge—now retired Sarge—to start their life together as a married couple, I knew I couldn't be spending nights and weekends chasing down bad guys.

My new role was more strategic and administrative, which allowed me to work fairly regular hours. I could be with Zoey on the weekends and attend her after-school activities. Having a flexible schedule meant I could come and go as I needed. But when Zoey blew out the candles on her 16th birthday cake and I handed her the set of car keys, I felt a physical sickness about what might happen to my daughter as she drove around, becoming more independent right before my eyes. I knew Zoey needed her mother, but in a different way. She needed me to be her emotional support, to continue to guide her and ensure her safety. But she didn't need me to drive her to Girl Scouts or basketball practice, soccer, or academic decathlon. She was growing up, and I had to adapt to that new reality.

"Shall we head over to the conference room?"

"Yeah, that would be great. Let me grab my laptop."

As I stepped toward the conference room, my cell phone buzzed. I stared at the screen and answered, "Hello?"

"Hi, Mom. I just wanted to tell you I'm leaving now to head over to babysit Audrey. Barney's been fed and walked, and he'll be happy to see you when you get home."

At least Barney still needed me. He was more than willing to hang out with me on Friday nights to watch movies and eat pizza. To be fair, Zoey was a great kid—a teenager, a young woman. But her Friday nights often involved football games or school dances or sleepovers. Barney and I had become two peas in a pod, or more accurately, two creatures sitting on the couch with only each other to hang out with. "Great. Tell Kim I said hello and to little miss Audrey, too."

As Zoey had always wanted, she was Audrey's favorite babysitter. Zoey adored Audrey, and since she was older, Zoey liked to do with Audrey all the things she used to do with Kim. They painted nails, put glitter on their faces and in their hair, and art projects were commonplace. I had to apologize to Kim and Hirsch on more than one occasion for all the glitter their house was now full of. Of course, they didn't mind.

"Okay. Love you, Mom. Bye."

"Love you too." She had already hung up. Zoey was always in a hurry and demanded to be on time.

With the phone tucked back in my pocket, I turned back to Vincent, who said, "That was Zoey, right? Is she heading over to Hirsch's?"

"Yes, she's babysitting Audrey."

"Babysitting Audrey. How do you feel about Zoey driving?"

"I've never been more terrified," I admitted.

Vincent chuckled and then playfully patted me on the shoulder. "Don't worry. She'll be fine. You have a tracking device on her car, right?"

"No, but I probably should."

"Well, you should definitely get one. And between the two of us, we could easily install it in her car. She wouldn't even know."

It wasn't a bad idea. Actually, I doubted Zoey would even mind. It would be just in case something went wrong or if somebody stole it. I tried to keep Zoey sheltered, but I knew all too well the monsters that lurked in the night.

I trusted Zoey. She was smart, cunning, and I had been taking her to self-defense classes since she was able. She was tough, but she was also a beautiful teenage girl, and I knew that was a beacon to the worst of the worst out there. "I might just take you up on that."

We trudged toward the conference room. Inside, Vincent said, "The couple that's coming in want to find their daughter. She's been missing for two years."

"Why aren't the police looking for her?"

"I talked to the mother on the phone. She said there was nothing they could do. They think she is a runaway, which, at first, Mrs. Kimble—that's the missing girl's mom—thought so too."

"Really?"

"Yeah, she didn't get into it on the phone, but she told me she'd explain everything when she gets here."

"Okay." It had been a hot minute since I'd worked a missing persons case. Not that Drakos Monroe didn't investigate missing persons, but these days, it was mostly security, whether for a visiting dignitary, a celebrity, or the wealthy.

My role had evolved into strategizing with the teams on how best to secure our clients. In addition, I also worked with victims and survivors of intimate partner violence, helping them leave abusive partners. It was my specialty and my primary role before I worked on cold cases with Hirsch. As such, I handled all of those cases firsthand. I would meet with each of the women and men to discuss the situation and come up with a plan to extract them and keep them safe. It was the most rewarding thing I'd ever done at Drakos Monroe Security & Investigations.

But I had to admit, I still missed the rush of the Cold Case Squad going in, catching bad guys, and watching Hirsch slap the silver handcuffs on them. And then the team would go out and celebrate another win. A part of me always hoped we would work together again. But it had been five years. He had accepted a new position, and so had I. I guess it wasn't meant to be.

The Polycom lit up. Vincent answered, "This is Vincent and Martina."

"Mr. and Mrs. Kimble are here," the voice from the other end said.

"Okay," Vincent replied. "Martina will go get them."

There were certain responsibilities that came along with having your name on the company sign. It always impressed people when the owner met them personally for the first intake meeting. I liked to sit in on the meetings with our investigators for the first time to assess how much help they may need. Most cases were simple, requiring just one investigator. But on occasion, we had a case that needed a team effort. That's where I came in to make the assessment. "I'll be back."

I hurried down to reception and smiled at Mrs. Pearson. Then I glanced over at a middle-aged couple dressed smartly, worry etched on their faces. "Hi, I'm Martina Monroe," I introduced myself, extending my hand.

The woman, with graying roots and pale blue eyes, took it.

"I'm Cynthia Kimble, and this is my husband, Louis," she replied.

After handshakes and business cards, I said, "I'll take you back to our conference room. My colleague Vincent Teller, one of our top investigators, is there. We'll go over the case and talk about a game plan to find your daughter."

Cynthia said, "Thank you so much," as I led them back to the conference room.

I asked if they needed a beverage, noting their nervousness. Most of our clients were on edge when they arrived. Not that they needed to be. They had hired us. We worked for them. Our goal was to keep them happy.

We walked into the conference room, where Vincent stood up. I introduced the Kimbles and offered them a seat.

"So, what can you tell us about your daughter?" Vincent asked.

Mrs. Kimble began, "The last time we saw Katie was two years ago. She was twenty, about to turn twenty-one, and told us she was dropping out of college and moving up north with her new boyfriend."

"Was it surprising that she was dropping out of school?" Vincent asked.

"Not really," Mrs. Kimble replied. "She was always a bit of a free spirit. Wanted to do her own thing. She was an artist. Katie said she was tired of capitalism and material goods and thought it was all a waste of energy."

Mr. Kimble interjected, "She never did a thing we asked her to do. We gave her everything, paid for college, car, braces... everything. She was ungrateful."

Mrs. Kimble shot her husband a glare. I wondered if their daughter's disappearance had taken a toll on their marriage or if it had always been strained. "Did she say where she was moving to?" I asked.

"Chico," Mrs. Kimble said. "She told us her boyfriend had a farm where they'd live off the land and live a more enlightened life. We begged her not to go. She told me she would keep in touch, but she never did. It was the last time we ever saw her... and that awful boyfriend."

"What can you tell us about the boyfriend?"

"I only met him a few times," Mrs. Kimble said. "But I didn't like him one bit. He was older, a lot older. He was probably early to mid-thirties. Too old. He had long hair and acted really smug, like he was better than everybody else. And he was always telling her what to do, but in a way that made it seem like she wanted it. I don't know how to explain it, but she seemed to do whatever he wanted, whenever he wanted it. I knew he was bad news."

"Have you tried to find her yourself?"

"We tried. We went to Chico and asked around, but everyone we spoke to had never heard of her or him or the farm," Mr. Kimble answered.

"What was his name?"

"He told us his name was Atlas, but I have a feeling it wasn't his real name," Mrs. Kimble said.

I watched as Vincent began typing, taking notes on everything Mr. and Mrs. Kimble were telling us. Unfortunately, my initial gut feeling said their fears were justified. "Do you have any reason to believe something bad has happened to Katie?"

"Just mother's intuition," Mrs. Kimble confessed. "I feel like I'm losing her, like if I don't do something, I'll never see her again."

Vincent scratched the side of his head. "She was a bit of a free spirit?"

Mrs. Kimble said, "She was."

"Was there a reason she didn't want to be at home with the two of you?" I inquired.

"She thought we were too controlling," Mr. Kimble said, folding his arms across his chest. "She told us she had free will, and we were trying to squash her spirit."

"Did your daughter have any friends who may have been in contact with Katie over the last two years?" Vincent asked.

"She had friends. Friends from high school," Mrs. Kimble replied. "I talked to them, and they said they haven't heard from Katie either. That's what's really made me nervous."

"We will need to have the names of those friends," Vincent said.

"Of course," Mrs. Kimble agreed.

"Did you bring a photograph of Katie?"

"Oh, yes. Vincent told us on the phone it was important to bring the most current photo of her. I also noted all the information about her vehicle, the classes she was taking before she dropped out of college, and everything we knew about Atlas, which wasn't much, just that he was no good. He seemed a little rough, you know?" Mrs. Kimble said.

Unfortunately, I understood all too well. A young, idealistic woman got caught up with a charismatic older man whom she followed unquestioningly. It was definitely a recipe for disaster. I only prayed we would find Katie alive.

Mrs. Kimble passed her packet of paper and the photographs of Katie across the table. Katie had strawberry-blonde hair, freckles, and big blue eyes. She looked like the all-American teen. In one photo, she wore daisies in her hair, a flower child in spirit and perhaps a little too trusting as well.

At the end of the meeting, I assured them, "We will do everything we can to find Katie," and I meant it.

BACK IN VINCENT'S CUBICLE, he asked, "What do you think, boss? Will we find her?"

"I think so."

He gave me a knowing smile. "We always find them. I'd like to think there's nothing we can't do together, Martina."

Oh, boy, Vincent's on one today. "For now, you can take the lead. Do all the background on both Katie and this Atlas person, and we'll start setting up interviews."

"Are you working this one with me?" he asked, glee in his eyes.

"Yeah, I think it would be a good idea. At least in the beginning, to get a better idea of how this might unfold."

"Do you think she's still alive?" Vincent questioned.

"Given the description of the boyfriend, I'm worried she may not be. And if this boyfriend did something to her, he's dangerous. Which means this case could be dangerous and backup is always a good thing. No case is worth dying over."

"Hundred percent agree, boss."

My mind drifted, and I wasn't sure what I was feeling in that moment. Perhaps nostalgia or a sixth sense the case was bigger than it appeared. It got me thinking about all kinds of things—the past, the present, the future. What would it all lead to?

3
____

HIRSCH

My phone rang as I spotted Jayda and Ross heading toward my office. I lifted a finger to let them know I needed a minute. Answering the call, I said, "Hey. What's up?"

"Hi. Just wanted to let you know Zoey's here. I plan to go to the gym, get ready for dinner, and meet you at the restaurant at six?"

"Sounds great."

"How's work?"

Glancing up at my two detectives, I said, "Calm waters."

"That's good to hear."

In the background, I could hear Audrey chatting with Zoey. At five years old, Audrey talked nonstop. When I first met Zoey, she was seven, and I thought, *wow, that girl can talk.* She fired off questions a mile a minute. Audrey was full of that same energy and at times left me exhausted. "Can I say hi to Audrey?"

"Sure, give me a sec."

After some muffled noises, I heard the sweetest voice. "Hi, Daddy."

"Hi, Audrey, how's your day going?"

"It's great! Zoey just got here. I can't wait to play with her. She brought me some new glitter. It's rainbow colored. It's got all the colors of the rainbow. Can you believe it?"

Glitter was everywhere. I never thought my life would be filled with so much darn glitter. I also didn't think I'd be the guy sitting behind a desk. Things change, life changes, and I knew it would the moment I saw my daughter's blue eyes staring up at me, asking me to protect her, to love her, and to be there for her. "That sounds amazing. Okay, I have to go. Love you, Audrey."

"I love you too, Daddy."

The little girl turned me to mush every time. Kim returned to the line. "Okay, I'll see you at six."

"Can't wait. Love you."

"Love you too."

As much as I loved my daughter, I loved my wife too, and getting one night a week to spend time with just her was always a highlight.

I waved Jayda and Ross inside. "What's going on?"

"We just got back from talking to a couple of CIs. We think we have a visual on who sold drugs to our last victim."

The team was tracking a drug organization selling LSD laced with fentanyl to teens and college kids in the suburbs. Our theory was the victims were unaware the drugs were laced with fentanyl. In order to stop future fatalities, I put together a team comprised of homicide and narcotics officers to end it before more people lost their lives after seeking a recreational high. "Do you have a description?"

"Our confidential informant, one of our best CIs, told us where our guy is selling the drugs. We want to do a stakeout tonight. See if we can get photos and proof he's dealing. And maybe learn who his regulars are and question them. We don't want to spook the perp, street name, Zan the Man. We want to be sure he's connected before questioning him. Don't want to tip him off we know he's dealing the deadly tabs."

"How credible is the tip?"

"The CI told us he's seen the same guy selling little baggies with orange sun stickers affixed to them—the same stickers found with the victims. Apparently, they're calling the drugs Sunny D. Our guy doesn't usually start dealing until after dark. But we need approval for the OT. Preferably for a few nights. This might be our big break."

When I learned Sarge, or Ted, planned to retire, I considered the position. It turned out Sarge had already given my name to the brass. It was a logical fit. I could still work with one of the greatest teams imaginable, minus a few key players like Martina and Vincent. Things were certainly different, quieter, and a little less dangerous than the days of the Cold Case Squad.

"I'll approve the overtime."

"Thanks, boss," Ross said with a wink.

"Hey, do you know if Vincent and Martina will be at the barbecue next weekend?" Jayda asked.

"Martina and her crew will be there, and Vincent said he was coming, but he wasn't sure if Amanda could make it."

"I haven't seen her in a few months. Hope she's doing all right. You talk to her much?" Jayda asked.

Sounded like I wasn't the only one who missed Martina. "We talk. She's doing well. Just became a sponsor."

"She must have some extra time on her hands, now that Zoey's behind the wheel."

"She does. But she seems happy." The thought of Audrey driving at sixteen sent shivers down my body.

"Could she be happier?" Jayda said, implying maybe she could be. "I've been thinking about her because I know someone who might be a good match for her."

Raising my hands, I said, "That's between you and Martina. I'm not getting in the middle of that."

Jayda laughed. "Fair enough. I'll bring it up at the barbecue, or I could bring him as a plus one and introduce them?"

It might be entertaining to watch Jayda try to convince Martina to go on a date with her friend. Not that I didn't think Martina deserved a special someone in her life, but forcing anything on Martina was a bad idea. Who knew? It could be a good fit. Stranger things had happened. "Extra plus one granted."

Ross smirked. "I can't wait to see this."

"I guess I can cancel the entertainment."

"Well, if nothing else, I'll be saving you a few bucks," Jayda teased.

"You have my gratitude."

"Take care, boss."

I waved as the two exited my office.

Things certainly were different. We all felt the hole Martina and Vincent left in the CoCo County Sheriff's office. Not that there was a Cold Case Squad anymore. Most of the team went to homicide, the rest to narcotics. We no longer had dedicated services just for us and had less interaction with Kiki from the forensics lab and the research team. The change was good; it brought me a beautiful wife and child and a life worth living outside of the job. But sometimes, I wished I could have them and the Cold Case Squad too. I thought, *You can have it all, just not all at once.*

4

———

FERN

Awakened in a cold sweat, I quickly propped myself up and wiped my brow with the edge of the sheet. Worried about the consequences of what I'd done, I wondered if I'd spend the rest of my life in prison, and, more importantly, would my soul be locked in a dark place forever?

When Opal had joined the community, she said there was no one on the outside who cared for her. Not really, anyway. A vegetarian and lover of all creatures, Opal said the farm seemed like the perfect place for her.

She had met Atlas at a coffee shop, and he charmed her into hearing about our way of life. It was how he met several members, and I wondered how accidental the meetings really were. Atlas had a way of making one feel special, warm, and comforted—as if everything he said must be the truth. We all believed him. Maybe that was because we wanted so badly to have faith in something bigger than ourselves.

When Opal wandered onto the farm in her Birkenstocks and flowing patchwork skirt, I knew she'd be one of us. In some ways, she was, at first. She reminded me of myself, and I think that was why the situation felt so awful. She could be me and I could be her.

Like me, Opal was captivated by the rows and rows of vegetables, the loving atmosphere, and the common belief system that we were all there to support our earth, to love animals, and each other. When she learned how we paid for it all, she became a problem, and I was ashamed to admit that I understood the problem she posed for our community.

I'd explained the situation and that there was no need to be concerned, but I failed to take the shock out of her eyes or prevent her from cowering away from my embrace. It wasn't the reaction I'd hoped for. I pleaded with her to see it my way. But did she listen? No, she didn't. She cried, and she screamed, and then I did something I never thought I would do. I gave her a little something in her tea to calm her into a deep slumber. And for a little while, the quiet returned to our community.

Atlas and I had a conversation about what to do with her. I tried to convince him I could turn her back to us, to our way. I would keep her quiet. I would make her see that everything we were doing was okay—it was for all of us. We were a family.

He gave me a week.

Well, in that week, she only fought harder. She even tried to run away, to go to the police and destroy us. I convinced her to come back. I told her I would run away with her, that I believed everything she said was true and agreed we had simply lost our way.

It was then I managed to regain her trust. With that deception, I led her by the hand into a grove of redwood trees. I smiled and said, "Oh, look, a squirrel! He has a nut."

Her eyes lit up, and she turned, but there was no squirrel.

It was in that moment I grabbed the gun from my sling bag and aimed it at the back of her head. My hands trembled, and as she turned around, presumably to tell me she couldn't see the squirrel, her eyes met mine. Terrified of my own capabilities, I squeezed my eyes shut and pulled the trigger.

The sound of her falling to her knees was like the echo of a thick book landing on an old wooden floor, reverberating through a silent room.

She didn't die right away.

It took a good few minutes, but when I was sure her life was gone, I pulled her into the grave I'd dug earlier that morning and had covered with branches.

Premeditated.

First degree.

The look in her eyes—hurt, betrayal, and shock. My mind would never escape the image.

It was the first time I'd ever killed another living being. I had become a vegan in high school, eating no animal products—no butter, no cheese, no eggs—and I didn't wear leather. I believed all creatures big and small were sacred.

That was who I used to be.

Yes, Opal had threatened our way of life, but she was still a person. Now, I was haunted by her memory, the look in her eyes, and I couldn't help but wonder how I arrived here.

More importantly, why did he insist I was the one to kill her?

It made me wonder if he was testing me. If he was, I had passed, but at what cost? Nightmares filled my dreams and a sick feeling in my stomach was present all the time. I now questioned everything. Like all the people Atlas had claimed left the farm. Had they gone their own way, or did he kill them? Or had someone else killed them?

I didn't want to do it.

He told me it had to be me. I was the only one she trusted enough to lure her to her death. He was the leader, and I was his second in command, not his equal. Despite my pleas, promising

I could bring her to the spot and somebody else could do the deed, he said it was too risky. Atlas claimed he knew I could do it because I believed in our way of life and wanted to protect it. He'd said, "Darling. This is just a minor event in our lives. I love you, and you love me. Love conquers all."

What a fool I was.

How many people had he killed? How many people were buried in our sanctuary, our little piece of heaven? When we first met, I thought I was the luckiest woman in the world. He believed in what I believed in. He seemed so genuine and so different from any other man I'd ever met.

He took me away and said he'd take care of me, and together we would take care of everyone. We'd all take care of each other. But it wasn't until he ordered me to kill Opal that I realized he was everything I had been running away from. I was just too thick to realize it.

I was baffled at how he had convinced me murder was okay, that all of this was for the greater good. But how could it be? How could murdering a human be for the greater good? It was a lie, and I fell for it. I glanced over at him, sleeping beside me peacefully, with not a care in the world.

The tears streamed down my cheeks as I realized I couldn't live like that anymore. I had to break away, but how? I'd seen what happened to those who tried to leave, those who might bring the whole thing down. It was so strange how one moment, or one day, or one year, you could believe everything was a certain way. And then, in an instant, everything could look so different. What once was a rainbow of color now seemed brutally black and white.

Escape was my only option. It was only a matter of time before he'd come for me. He would sense my disapproval, my unhappiness. Atlas had a way of doing that; he always knew what I was thinking, what I was feeling.

In this new black and white world, I realized he'd known it all along. He knew every button to push and every word to say to make me believe in him. I was such a fool. But the worst part was, it had taken me this long to realize it.

He stirred, and my heart raced. I slid under the covers and pretended to be asleep.

5

MARTINA

VINCENT SCRIBBLED FURIOUSLY on the whiteboard in my office. When he was done, he turned around and said, "I finished the initial background on Katie Kimble."

Reading the notes, I saw he had confirmed there had been no social media posts and no movement on her cell phone or her bank accounts. "What you're telling me is there's been no trace of Katie over the last two years?"

"Exactly. I searched all records that are available online."

This didn't bode well for Katie and her parents. No trace of Katie in two years likely meant she was hiding out for some unknown reason or she was dead. I had hoped the case wouldn't end with a body. I didn't miss performing death notifications to parents, grandparents, and loved ones like I had at the CoCo County Sheriff's Department. My gut was telling me the case needed at least two resources because if Katie was murdered, her boyfriend or the killer who we'd be hunting was dangerous.

"Did you find any new friends or family who we don't already have in the notes from her parents?"

"I found the social media accounts for the friends her

parents provided names for. So, we can definitely interview them in person to get some details on the boyfriend."

It was critical we found the boyfriend. My gut told me if we found him, we would find Katie.

"Any sign of Atlas on social media?"

Vincent raised his finger and said, "Aha! But of course."

Although Vincent had aged over the last five years, his zest for life hadn't. He was more calm, but the theatrics remained. Vincent reminded me of Zoey in some ways; he had that sparkle some people had, a wide-eyed optimism.

"Did you get a picture of the boyfriend?"

"Yep." He walked back over to the whiteboard and wrote the name Atlas. "Our friend Atlas doesn't have any social media presence or any records in his name. It's kind of unusual, right?"

It was peculiar. "Could both Katie and her boyfriend be dead or on the run together?"

"Sure. It's odd, though. So, of course, I dug a little further."

"And?"

"Well, I ran our friend Atlas's photo, thanks to Katie's social media page, through background, and guess what?" he asked, brows raised.

"His name is not Atlas?"

"That's why you're the boss."

"Did you get a name?"

"I did. After running his face through the handy-dandy facial recognition software, I matched it up with a DMV photo. Want to guess what his real name is?"

Unsure if it was my age, the fact I had less on my plate, or that I had a teenager in the house forcing me to have more compassion and acceptance, I was more patient—even for Vincent's drama. It was how I knew I was ready to be a sponsor, to help somebody who needed me. I wanted to be someone to lend a hand when my sponsee stumbled or fell and needed to be picked back up. "No idea. What's his name?"

"Jackson Galen is the legal name of our pal, Atlas."

"Well, that's a start." I eased out of my chair and met Vincent at the whiteboard. "Okay, so Katie's boyfriend was going by an alias, which isn't all that strange; some people like to have nicknames. So, what do we know about Jackson Galen?"

"He has a driver's license, car insurance, cell phone, but no employment records for the last ten years."

"Did you get an address?"

"I did."

Most investigators like myself would've led with that—the fact that we had the address of the boyfriend of our missing person. But we were dealing with Vincent.

"Do we know if it's current?"

"Well, that, my friend, is where we come in. He's listed as the property owner, so he likely still lives there, unless he's renting it out. My thought was we go check it out."

"Where's the address?"

"Up north on the coast, in a town called Jenner. I looked online; it's a beautiful coastal town."

"Sounds expensive."

"Depends on if you want ocean views. If you do, it'll cost you, but the hillside is more affordable. A lot less than in the Bay Area."

"Did you check out if he's in the mountains or on the coast?"

"Of course. I can map it like nobody's business. He's on the hillside. But don't let that fool you. Property records say it's twenty acres."

I glanced at the Timex on my wrist. "Nice work. What else do you know? Does he have family in the area?"

"Family is on the East Coast."

"Was he born on the East Coast?"

Vincent grimaced. "Didn't check birth records."

It wasn't standard but not a bad idea. I liked to know everything about a potential suspect. Especially if the suspect may have killed our missing person. "I'd like to talk to Atlas or Jackson Galen, whatever he likes to be called. It'll take us about two hours to get to the property. Maybe we ought to head out now. It would be nice to close this one quickly."

And to ease Katie's parents' suffering. I couldn't imagine what it would be like to not hear from Zoey in two years. The girl had talked nonstop since she muttered, "mama" as a baby. Two years not knowing if she was okay? It would eat me up. We needed to find out what happened to Katie, and fast. Mr. and Mrs. Kimble needed answers, and I fully intended to deliver them.

"Since he may be a murderer, should we bring backup? I mean, you're awesome but..."

It was a fair point. Especially if Atlas was dangerous and could hide out on twenty acres. "I'll ask a few members of the security team if they're available to be our lookout. The area is pretty remote, and we could easily disappear without a trace."

And I wasn't naïve enough to think that murderers didn't keep other murderers' company. Assuming our suspect was a suspect and not just innocently living his best life on the coast.

Vincent said, "Sounds like a plan, boss."

Every time Vincent called me boss, I couldn't help but think of Hirsch and a different time. Stavros and I had offered Hirsch a spot in the private sector, but he said he was born to wear the badge. We couldn't argue with that, but it didn't mean I hadn't wished Hirsch would reconsider. Shaking the thoughts out of my head, I refocused on the task at hand, finding Katie Kimble.

6

———

MARTINA

Taking in the ocean views along the winding highway, I contemplated what it would be like to live in such a beautiful place. The Bay Area was great, but I lived in the suburbs. It was nice, and we had plenty of hiking trails to explore on the weekends. Climbing up the mountains, more like hills, and overlooking the bay or the city lights was incredible. But this... this was like God had painted a picture of what heaven would look like on earth, and this was it.

Gorgeous redwoods on one side of the road and miles and miles of ocean on the other—there wasn't a more breathtaking scene. Maybe Katie wasn't dead. Maybe she'd simply wanted a different life, one away from the city and the hustle and bustle of the Bay Area. Her parents said she wanted to be an artist. What better place to go than somewhere you'd be surrounded by nature on all sides? Maybe she'd eschewed social media and the Internet and was living amongst Mother Nature.

I could understand that. Our constant connection to our computer screens was such a habit I could no longer imagine what life would be like without them. Maybe it would be glorious.

It seemed too easy to jump to the idea that Katie was dead and that her boyfriend was terrible and had murdered her. But then again, if she simply wanted another kind of life, why would she never contact her parents or her friends? Maybe they weren't as happy a family as they led us to believe. Or she was simply a rebellious young woman who thought her parents were part of a toxic, stressful world where there was traffic and hordes of people and everywhere you looked there was crime, drugs, and the worst parts of society.

Looking at the scenery, I held on to hope for Katie. Maybe she wasn't dead. Maybe we'd find her thriving. Wouldn't that be great to report back to her parents? It would be heartbreaking still—imagine your own child not wanting to talk to you for two years. The thought made my heart hurt.

Vincent pointed. "It's the turn right up there."

The road curved upward, surrounded by giant trees, mostly redwoods, bushes, and other greenery. It was paradise.

"The map says it's about half a mile on the left."

As we approached the property, there was a wooden gate barring us from driving up to the front door. If this were in the Bay Area, I'd be suspicious, wondering why they had a gate. Were they trying to keep people out or keep people in? We had passed several gates just like it on the drive up. Perhaps the gate was there to designate land ownership lines or to give a sense of grandeur.

"Let's park up the hill and go on foot. Can you call the team and let them know to park on a side street? We don't want it to look like they're with us. We'll circle back and park nearby."

"You got it, boss."

Adrenaline filled my veins. It had been ages since I'd been out in the field looking for a missing person. I really hoped I could bring a happy ending to Katie's family, and I was ready to pound the pavement, or in this case, scour the forest floor to do so.

With everyone in position, I parked and hopped out of the car. Vincent followed behind. My boots crunched on the gravel that led to the driveway. There weren't any "No Trespassing" signs. Maybe they didn't need them in this area? People knew better? Or people were respectful of other people's property lines.

We made it about two feet across the property line when, from what seemed like out of nowhere, but I quickly realized there was a path to the left, a man wearing linen pants and a white T-shirt with long, flowing dark hair said, "Can I help you?"

I glanced around and looked up to see if our security team saw the man. A slight rustling in the trees, and I knew they had eyes on us.

"Are you Atlas?"

"No, my name is Sage."

"We're here to see Atlas."

"I'm afraid he's not here right now."

"But he lives here?" I asked, and the man nodded slightly. He didn't seem suspicious, other than the speed at which he greeted us. "Do you know when he'll be back?"

"Hard to say. He went out for supplies."

The only number listed for Jackson Galen was a cell phone, and he hadn't picked up when we called. We knew there was a potential we had driven for two hours and wouldn't be able to talk to him. I guessed it was too much to ask for a little luck in the case. "Do you know Katie? Is she here?"

The man cocked his head. "I don't know anybody named Katie."

As he spoke, I heard footsteps coming from the path on the left. It was a woman. She wore a similar outfit—linen pants and a matching linen top. Her chestnut hair flowed, with big brown eyes, and a soft face covered in freckles. She looked at Sage, who said, "They're looking for Atlas."

She said, "He went out for supplies."

"That's what I told them," Sage added.

"And what is your name?" I asked the woman.

She smiled brightly. "My name is Cloud."

"My name is Martina, and this is my partner, Vincent. We're looking for Atlas to talk to him about a friend of ours. Her name is Katie. Do you know Katie?"

With a simple shake of her head, she said, "No, I don't know anybody named Katie."

They seemed sincere, and I didn't pick up on any tells that they were lying, like covering their mouth or eyes or fidgeting. Their voices remained steady.

"Do you both live here?" I inquired.

Sage said, "Yes, Cloud and I have been here for almost three years now."

"How many people live here?" I asked.

Cloud smiled again. "We have quite a few. I think there's almost twenty of us now. It's so beautiful here; people just keep wanting to move in."

"Is this a commune?"

Sage said, "Yes. It's so incredible. We live off the land, go on hikes. There's not a more beautiful place on earth."

He wasn't wrong about that. "May I show you a photo of our friend Katie and see if she's been here, maybe just visiting?"

"Of course. We'll do anything we can to reconnect you with your loved one," Cloud assured us.

Vincent said, "We appreciate that." From his bag, he pulled out an 8 x 10 of Katie and handed it to Sage.

Cloud huddled close to inspect the photo. They both studied the image. Cloud rocked her head from side to side.

"She looks familiar, but she wasn't here. Her name is Katie?"

"Yes," I confirmed.

"Well, unfortunately, we haven't seen her. If we ever do, can we call you? We don't have telephones here on the property, but we could head into town."

"Yes, that would be appreciated." I pulled out a business card from inside my jacket and handed it over. Sage accepted it and read it intently, much like he had studied the photo.

"Drakos Monroe Security and Investigations. Are you a private investigator?"

"Yes. Katie's a family friend. Her parents are quite worried about her; they haven't seen her in two years."

Cloud clutched her chest. "I can't imagine being without my child for two years. Good luck in finding her."

"I can't either. Thank you for your time."

Vincent and I bid our goodbyes and headed back to the car. A prickling on the back of my neck stopped me at the door. I turned and glanced over my shoulder. Cloud and Sage were watching us intently, not moving from the spot we had left them. It was strange, as if they didn't get many visitors from the outside. I waved again and climbed into the car before heading down the road as if I were done with their address. But I certainly wasn't. More than ever, my gut told me I needed to speak with Atlas.

7

———

FERN

At least I was off the compound, but I was still with Atlas. He hadn't done anything that made me think he suspected my true thoughts. He believed in a higher being, but he didn't say he was one, which was why I had trusted him when he told me I could live a better life where no modern technology could cut down my creativity. I wouldn't have to be bombarded by news and media that made me depressed, thinking the world was a dark, dark place that could never be restored.

Atlas promised me a world of communal living that honored the earth and each other. He said he was trying to recreate the idea of an enlightened world, like so many back in the 1960s. He preached free love, not like sex orgies all the time, but loving each other, the earth, the wind, the fire, the land, the sun. It all sounded so amazing, and I fell for every word because when he brought me to his property, it was all there. Rows of crops, people wearing comfortable clothing, no makeup, and no pretension. It was truly everything I'd ever imagined, and I didn't see any fault with it. I didn't see any reason to question the true purpose of the community Atlas built. Part of me still believed it was the life he strived to live, but his inconsistency gave me pause.

Like the fact he lied. To me. He made promises of love and fidelity, but when I caught him with another woman in the act, right there in the community, his eyes met mine, and all he did was lift his hand and wave. I ran off in tears, unsure of what I'd seen, what I was feeling, and why he was so calm about the whole thing. He waited two hours to come find me. And when he did, he looked me right in the eyes, and said, "Darling. Why are you upset?"

Through tears, I said, "You told me we were partners. That I was special and your only one! You told me we shared a spirit."

"You have me. All the parts that matter. You have my spirit, you have my heart. Sex, that's just a physical thing. I was simply sharing the gift of love. That other woman doesn't have me. You have me."

In that moment, I trusted he was sincere and that I'd misunderstood what his intentions were. I even concluded that his actions went along with his idea of free love; that we were just bodies, loving one another and the earth. But when I asked about my own actions, he said it was different. "How so?" I questioned, "If you get to exchange love as physical affection with other women, why can't I share physical affection with other men?"

"Because you are special," he replied. "I am the leader of this beautiful community, and you are my number one. You are an example of how to be a pure and beautiful being. I know that's who you are inside. You have this glowing light, this creativity, this love, this pure energy that I want people to feel. And if you share your physical love with everybody, it diminishes how special you are."

It made me feel important to hold that role in our community. After that, we smoked pot and fell asleep in each other's arms with smiles on our faces. Everything seemed right. But in reflection, I wondered if I had been making excuses for all of his actions. If we were anywhere else, I could see them for what they were—lies to keep me close.

What was I going to do?

After his first sharing of physical love, infidelity, with another woman, I hadn't understood it was going to happen again and so frequently. When I told him it bothered me, that I didn't feel special when he wanted to share his physical love with everyone and not just me, he was kind—at first. "Darling, don't be upset. I need you to accept this, embrace this gift and this role you have in our community."

By that point, he had been with a dozen women, some of whom were regular members of the community, some who just came in and out. Where they went—on the road, hiking, or back home, I didn't know. I never saw them again.

He dismissed my feelings, and it didn't feel right. "But if I'm so special, wouldn't you be faithful to me?"

His eyes grew dark, and he said, "This is how it has to be. I don't want you bringing it up again. I don't want to have to send you away."

My stomach clenched.

Send me away? Reflecting on that moment, I realized him sending me away may not have meant sending me home but sending me to another realm, to heaven or hell, or wherever we go after we die. How could I escape his clutches?

What happened to all the others he'd sent away, who didn't fall in line with the rules? And why wasn't I strong enough to leave when I knew something was wrong? In my gut, I knew, and I pushed it down and acted like it wasn't there. That persistent feeling had been nagging me the whole time. If I stayed in Atlas's world any longer, my insides would rot, and I might as well be dead.

8

———————

HIRSCH

In a small conference room, I met with Jayda, Ross, and Rosemary from our research team. Jayda said, "You remember Rosemary, right?"

"Yes, of course. It's good to see you, Rosemary."

Since I had taken on the role of sergeant, my interactions with the support staff at the sheriff's department had decreased. I no longer had daily conversations with the forensics team or the research team. It was mostly just the sheriff, the brass, and my investigators, which I loved, but it wasn't the same as being in the mix on a daily basis.

The upcoming barbecue was playing on my nostalgia for the days of the Cold Case Squad. Martina and Vincent had suggested an annual barbecue for the squad, and I, with Kim's urging, offered our back yard. I looked forward to it each year, and each year I longed for the old days, where we strategized how to break open a 20-year-old cold case, finally bringing answers to families that had waited far too long. But times changed, and if you don't change, well, you know what happened to the dinosaurs.

Don't get me wrong. Over the last five years, I worked with a few other departments, even other sheriff's departments, trying to gauge interest in opening up another cold case squad, finding funding for a much-needed team. But no takers. It was hard to argue with our sheriff. Since we lost our squad, our homicide closure rates skyrocketed because most of the best of the best, the old cold case squad, had been transferred into homicide.

The ability to work on cold cases was why I joined the CoCo County Sheriff's Department in the first place, the promise of being able to open and solve cold cases. In the back of my mind, I hoped one day the case we opened would be my brother's murder. Like other families, the Hirsches had waited a long time to learn the truth about what happened to Nick. The responding officers and the homicide detective back then said it was a mugging and that there were no witnesses. They took my brother's wallet and his car, but they never found either. Since becoming a homicide detective, I never wanted another family to ask why their loved one was taken from them and not get an answer. As a parent, I could only imagine what my parents went through. For me, losing my big brother was the most traumatic experience of my life.

"What did you find?" I asked.

Jayda said, "Last night, we spotted our dealer. We have photos of him participating in a few drug deals. We called in uniforms to get the buyers and confiscate the drugs—and maybe save their lives. I sent the photos over to narcotics. Kiva said he thinks our dealer was a juvenile offender but couldn't remember the name. Rosemary ran the photo through facial recognition. Sure enough, he popped up. The kid's name is Zander Jenkins."

"What's his story?"

"He just turned eighteen. Grew up in Oakland. No dad. Single mom. A bunch of brothers and sisters. Turned to the streets to make cash and get protection from local gangs. First arrest was at age twelve."

"He's still a kid."

Jayda said, "He is. We don't think he's the big fish."

Ross added, "Obviously. An 18-year-old is not making these drugs. We're guessing he's a low-level dealer."

Glancing over at Rosemary, sensing she had something to say, I said, "That's pretty much how it usually goes. Did you find something else?"

Rosemary said, "I reviewed the ME report on the three victims and the responding officers' notes. The witness statements were all about the same. They went to score LSD to party and then died. It's incredibly rare to overdose on LSD, so the friends who hadn't taken it yet suspected something was wrong and didn't take the drugs themselves. So, we have samples in evidence."

"Did Kiki test them?"

"She did. She thinks whoever is cooking the drugs messed up. They put too much fentanyl in them. The dealers add it to give the customers a better high for a lower price. You only need a tiny bit of fentanyl to get high, so it's cheap. But the cook likely messed up or wasn't careful and put too much of the extra ingredient."

"So, we have a drug dealer trying to provide a better experience for their customers, but they aren't very good at making drugs."

Her chin dipped in a nod. "Exactly." Rosemary continued, "Kiki said to make the tablets requires specialized equipment and skill. It's rare. So, we were talking, and we think it's important I research all parties capable of manufacturing the drugs. It could lead us to the drug organization."

Up to that point, the drug dealers were practically ghosts.

"Sounds like a good idea. What about you two? What's your plan?"

Jayda said, "Well, that's not all we found. During our surveillance, we spotted a sedan meeting up with Zander a few times. We think he was giving Zander more drugs to sell or collecting cash."

"Do we know who 'he' is?"

"Yep. We have photos and the license plate number. Our guy is Ashworth Dante. He's twenty-two and grew up in Pleasant Hill. No criminal record."

"Do you have a known address?"

"We talked to the property management company for the address associated with the vehicle registration. Ashworth hasn't lived there in a year. We don't know where he lives."

Ross added, "We plan to follow him and find out where he goes after they finish up for the night."

"Good. Maybe we'll get lucky and he'll lead you to the higher ups."

"That's what we're hoping. We'd like a second team to pick up Zander while we pursue Ashworth. Maybe two of our narcotics pals. Kiva says he and his partner can do it."

"Solid plan. Nice work."

The three sat quietly. "I'm guessing you need some OT?"

Jayda smiled widely. "Yep."

"Okay, I've got enough funding for overtime for the next week. Let's go at this hard. We have to get those drugs off the streets." We couldn't let any more kids die on our watch.

We chitchatted and said our goodbyes. I headed toward the coffeemaker, my mind wandering to the many conversations I'd had by this machine, mostly with Martina, the caffeine addict. She said it was the one vice she was allowed after becoming sober.

In my new role as sergeant, I was safe. I was not out in the field getting shot at, but it was a lonelier job. A lot of politics, working with the brass, just getting updates, and not being a part of the action. I missed that adrenaline rush and wondered if I had made the right choice.

9

———————

MARTINA

THE AROMA of freshly brewed coffee wafted through the café. I could certainly get used to Jenner, California. After placing my order, I stared out at the Russian River. It was calm, a slight breeze rippling the surface, with just a smattering of clouds in the sky. Such a different vibe than the Bay Area, where hustle and bustle was everyone's motto. Everybody was in a hurry, going somewhere. Nobody wanted to stop to say hello to a stranger because, well, we all read the news and strangers were dangerous.

Coffee in hand, Vincent and I met our security team on the deck, who had settled into the Adirondack chairs. Steve joked, "Could we hold all our meetings here?"

"Wouldn't that be nice?"

Vincent chimed in. "Why don't you have the company move headquarters out here? That would be awesome."

"Do you mind commuting?"

He smirked. "Point taken."

"What kind of vibe did you get from the two people you spoke to?" Steve asked.

"My first impression was that they're a couple of hippies living on a commune. No reason for them to lie."

Steve locked eyes with me. "And then?"

"And then, when they didn't let us out of their sight until we'd driven away, I thought maybe there was something there. Something gave me pause. What did you see?" I asked Steve and Otto.

Otto ran his hand over his beach-blond buzz cut. "Trees surround most of the property, making it difficult to see what's going on, but I could see the tops of several dwellings."

"Cloud and Sage told us there are twenty people living on the commune and they mostly live off the land."

"I'd say that sounds about right. There were enough dwellings for about twenty people to live there. And on twenty acres, they can grow all they want. Maybe that's what they're doing. Any whiff of marijuana?"

Shaking my head, I said, "I didn't smell anything. But that doesn't mean they weren't smoking or have their own farm, legal or illegal."

"That could explain why they watched you."

"It's possible, but that's not really our problem." If we were working with the CoCo County Sheriff's department, it would be a different story, and we'd be compelled to notify the narcotics team. But a hunch and a theory didn't warrant police intervention.

"Nope, we're just looking for Katie," Vincent confirmed.

Steve added, "One thing I thought was a little hinky was that they hurried toward you as soon as they heard the cars pull up, as if they were waiting for trespassers. It was a little weird."

Agreed. "It startled me how fast they appeared."

Otto said, "If I didn't know any better, I'd say they were the lookouts."

"But who are they looking out for? How many cops come around there?" I asked.

"Well, if they've got something to hide, they want to protect it."

Sipping my latte, I hummed to myself. It was good coffee. Excellent coffee, great scenery—I thought I'd just found my next vacation getaway.

"What's next, boss?"

"I say we give it a beat. Stick around, have some coffee. There are some bites in there too. Maybe have something to eat while we wait. We can go back and see if Atlas has returned. If he's innocent, he'll talk to us."

"And if he isn't?" Vincent asked.

"We'll have to work our powers of persuasion."

AN HOUR LATER, we returned to the property. Steve and Otto parked farther down the hill so the members of the commune wouldn't see their car. I parked right out front, acting as if I had nothing to hide, which I didn't.

Vincent and I approached, counting the steps from the car. One, two, three, four, five... By the fifth step, a person appeared. It wasn't Sage, but the man had a similar aesthetic—linen clothes, long hair, hemp bracelet. I flashed a wide smile and waved. "Hi, there."

"Hello. How can I help you?" he asked.

If I hadn't been convinced before that they were always watching for visitors, I was now. I wasn't entirely sure if there was something to be suspicious of, but they had certainly piqued my curiosity. "This is my partner, Vincent. We were here earlier. We're looking for Atlas."

He said, "Yes, Sage told me you dropped by. Unfortunately,

Atlas hasn't returned. Usually, it can take several hours to run errands. We're so far out here."

"I suppose getting supplies would take all day."

"It usually does."

Trying to butter him up, I said, "I'm not familiar with the area. Is the weather always this pleasant?"

"Oh, yeah, we've got the greatest weather. It's never too cold and never too hot. It's perfection."

That was my sentiment while we drove up the coast. "Sage and Cloud explained you grow vegetables and live off the land."

"Yes, it's incredible how much Mother Nature gives us if we treat her right."

"May we leave a message for Atlas, so he can call us when he returns?"

He laughed as if I'd said a joke. "Oh, I don't think that's possible. Here in our community, we've cut ties with worldly goods such as technology, telephones, and computers. We prefer a simpler life."

"But you have vehicles?" I asked. According to the records we found, Atlas, or Jackson Galen, owned a vehicle and a cell phone that was active. Did the other members of the community know about his cell phone?

"Yes, of course. And if we weren't so far out here, we'd ride bicycles. It's not perfect, but we do everything we can. Most of us came here as an escape from a world that wasn't right for us."

"I can understand that. I've seen a lot of bad things in my line of work."

"I'm sure you have. Atlas usually returns within the day. You could come back tomorrow."

"I'll do that. While I have you here... I'm sorry, I didn't catch your name?"

"My name is Forrest."

"It's nice to meet you, Forrest. We're also looking for a friend. Her name is Katie."

Vincent lifted the photo up and showed it to Forrest. "Have you ever seen her before?"

Forrest swallowed hard and stared at the photo. He placed his fingers on his chin, slightly covering his lips, and said, "No, I've never seen her before."

"How long have you lived here?"

His hand fell away, and Vincent placed Katie's photo back into his backpack. "Just over a year."

"That's great. Well, Forrest, I must admit I'm jealous of your way of life."

With a smugness, he said, "It is to be envied."

"Thank you for your help."

"Goodbye now. Be well."

"You too." I waved.

Vincent and I turned back to the vehicle and hopped inside. Like our last visit, the commune member kept his eyes on us until we had driven away. I had to wonder what they were hiding and why he acted nervous when he saw Katie's photo. Maybe she had been there? If so, why wouldn't he tell us? Maybe their fight for privacy had nothing to do with Katie. Many people had secrets—secrets they would do anything to keep buried. They could keep their secrets. I was only interested in finding Katie.

10

———

FERN

Assuming the role of my life, I strolled through the compound, waving at Cloud, Sage, and Soleil as they tended to the garden. They waved back, but their smiles were absent—an unusual occurrence. The community was almost always friendly with one another; we all had a common purpose. However, worry clouded their eyes, and I wondered why.

Sage stood up, removing his gardening gloves, and approached Atlas and me. "Atlas, Fern, happy to see you've returned. Do you need help to unload the car?"

"Yes, it's open," Atlas responded.

"There is something that happened while you were gone," Sage announced.

Panic gripped me, and I froze, as did Atlas. Was it the police? Were they coming for me? Had they discovered what I had done? The most vile thing one person could do to another... I had shot her in cold blood. Her eyes haunted me every time I shut my eyes.

"What happened?" Atlas inquired, breaking the silence.

"There was a man and a woman who came here looking for you," Sage began, retrieving a business card from his pocket. "A private investigator and her partner. They were looking for you and for a woman..." He paused, staring into my eyes before continuing. "A woman named Katie."

"What did you tell them?" Atlas asked, his tone level.

"That we've never seen Katie, and you were out running errands."

"Good," Atlas responded, looking unfazed.

Something was brewing inside me, something that I feared would bubble up and I wouldn't be able to contain. Atlas waved over Cloud and Forrest. "Please retrieve the supplies from the car. Once you're done bringing them into the common room, please meet me in my office." Without question, they scurried off, obeying his commands.

Everyone knew to obey Atlas; he had given us enough examples to know we had to toe his line. The first time I'd seen him strike another member of the community, I was horrified. I'd gasped and asked what he was doing. "We need order in our community. Without order, it's chaos," he had responded, his words etching into my memory.

The man's offense was minor; he'd stepped on the garden. High on drugs, he had stumbled into a patch. It was a complete accident, and we were high most of the time, so I didn't understand why Atlas was so upset. But he was. The first time I saw the violence, I was shocked. But when I watched it unfold for the second time, I was horrified.

There was a woman, one with whom he shared his physical love. She'd cried, confessing that she was worried she was pregnant. He had told her to be quiet and to stop being hysterical. He glanced at me, but I simply looked away. As the woman cried in front of our cabin, he raised his voice. "There will be no tears, and there will be no baby. Do you understand?"

Her response was barely audible, her voice shaking as she whispered, "Never... I'd never kill my baby." She cried again, and he smacked her across the face. The impact was so hard it made me jump. Those were the first instances of violence, but they certainly weren't the last. If a member of the community disobeyed too many times and threatened chaos upon our community, he dealt with them. For such actions, you were exiled and made an example of. I didn't know how far the example had gone.

Once Forrest and the others had scrambled out to bring in the supplies, we retreated to his office, and he said, "We need to contain this," his voice stern.

"What should I do?"

"Make it stop. We can't have outsiders coming into the community." With that, he continued toward his office two structures away from our home. I had to run to catch up.

Once inside, I asked, "How do we make it stop?"

With darkened eyes, he said, "Well, you took care of our last problem."

My eyes widened, and he must've seen the shock on my face. I couldn't kill another person and would die myself before I took another life.

"Don't worry, we'll think of something. I love you, Fern. I just don't want anything happening to you." He pulled me into a loving embrace, and despite my growing hate for him, his warmth still comforted me. It was a sensation I couldn't push away. Why did I still want his body next to mine?

My brain was so messed up. I knew what was right and wrong, and my gut was telling me to run, but I didn't know how I could escape and survive.

I wanted to leave the community behind, to go back to my old life. It wasn't perfect, but I didn't kill people. Had I become a horrible person? Was I always? Maybe a little rebellious, one who saw things a different way, but without Atlas, it never would have occurred to me to commit murder. He glared at me, pushing me back as he said, "We need this problem to go away."

Hesitantly, I suggested, "Well, maybe you should talk to them. Give them a story, make them go away. Show them the property and they'll see we're simply a loving community living off the land. They might give up and go away."

He scratched the side of his head and studied me from head to toe. "That's not a bad idea. We'll call a meeting with the others, explain the situation, and discuss how to treat our guests." A knock on the door diverted his attention. "Who is it?" he called out.

"It's Sage and Forrest," came the response.

He walked over and opened the door, inviting them in. "Tell us everything the man and woman said to you," he instructed.

After they finished, he turned to me and said, "Your plan is solid. When they return, we'll be welcoming and show them our community. But it won't be you leading them."

Of course, it wouldn't be me. "Good plan," I responded.

"We can plan for you to go on a hike when they return. We'll create a signal. You like to hike with Cloud, right?" he suggested.

"Of course. She's wonderful."

"It's decided then. We'll welcome our new friends with open arms."

"Great," I responded, trying to keep my voice steady.

Turning to Sage and Forrest, Atlas said, "Let's talk details," but then stopped and said to me, "You can go now."

With relief, I quickly left his office. It was at that moment I realized when he had promised I was his number one, was devoted to me, and had given me his heart and soul, I had in return given him my obedience. He controlled my every move. How had I not seen it before? And why had I let him?

11

____

MARTINA

Sunlight streamed through the green leaves high in the trees. It was early, just after sunrise, but I had a feeling we weren't too early. If what the community members—Cloud, Forrest, and Sage—had said was true, Atlas should have returned from running errands and getting supplies. If their way of life was to live off the land, my guess was they also rose at sunrise and wound down as the sun did the same.

Sure enough, within a few steps onto the property, in front of the wooden gate, Sage appeared from the path that led deep into their land. He smiled widely. "Martina Monroe and your partner, Vincent. Welcome back."

Why was he so friendly? We had assumed they were hiding something, and that was the reason for their attentive security. Was it simply they were afraid of outsiders or didn't want anyone tarnishing the world they had created?

"Good morning, Sage. I figured you would be an early riser."

"Absolutely, but you caught us right before we were to begin our morning yoga. You're welcome to join us."

Vincent and I looked at one another, and I said, "We're not really dressed for it."

"I understand. Perhaps we could shift the start of our yoga session. I let Atlas know you were calling for him. He's more than happy to meet with you."

This was a surprising turn of events. He was happy to meet us? Had we been all wrong about the strange, older boyfriend who we had assumed to be controlling and possibly abusive?

"That's great to hear."

"Please come with me." He unlatched the gate and swung it open.

Vincent and I walked through, and he shut the gate behind us. Before we could step onto the trail that everybody seemed to pop out of, a man with flowing dirty blonde hair, big blue eyes, and a scruffy beard waved. "You must be Martina and Vincent," he said with glee in his eyes as he raised his arms in a welcoming gesture.

"Yes. Are you Atlas?"

"I am. I'm so sorry I missed you yesterday. Please, what questions can I answer for you? I'm assuming you've come quite a way to talk to me. Can I get you anything? We have some wonderful iced tea we set out in the sun for five hours. It's delightful with fresh lemons that are grown right here on our property."

That *did* sound delightful. I turned to look at Vincent, who shrugged. "That sounds great."

Atlas waved us over to the path and said, "Come with me to the kitchen. I can give you a tour of the property if you'd like. Forrest was telling me you were quite impressed with our way of life."

Was he trying to recruit us to their commune? Could I resist? Maybe not, but I believed Zoey would absolutely resist.

"Yes, the idea of living in such a beautiful area, with the ocean just a hop over the highway—it's breathtaking. Eating what you grow sounds incredible."

"It is, it really is."

Soon, we were on the tree-lined path that kept the rest of the property private. We emerged, and my mouth dropped open, my eyes wide. There were wildflowers and herbs growing throughout the grounds, outdoor fire pits, multiple structures, greenhouses. Most spectacular as we approached the center was a large vegetable garden filled with squash, tomatoes, and peppers. Trees towered over the compound, and beyond the trees, I could see a redwood fence likely keeping unwanted visitors out. "It's stunning."

"It is. And as you can see, on top of all of our homes, we have solar panels. We use all solar energy to power our life. Mother Nature provides. It's incredible."

A few people wearing neutral-colored clothing, probably cotton or linen, waved at us with smiles on their faces.

"How long have you had this property?" I asked.

"I purchased it about ten years ago and began building and gathering like-minded individuals to help me build, cultivate the land, and live the life we all wanted but couldn't have back in the city, with all the people, the traffic lights, and the 'rush, rush, rush' mentality. Here, we focus on getting back to the earth and enjoying each other's company, loving one another. There's really not a better place on earth."

Did he believe in non-earthly places? Did he think he was a supreme being? Was this a cult? Was that the reason for the secrecy?

"Let's head to the building over there. We have a communal kitchen for everyone to use. We have multiple structures for people to have some privacy, of course. We like to cook together and be together, but there is no pressure if one needs alone time."

We stepped inside the structure. There was a gorgeous kitchen with a stainless-steel range and a set of ovens with beautiful wood cabinets. It surprised me it wasn't more rustic. "It's gorgeous. The wood on the cabinets is unique. I've never seen anything like it."

"All reclaimed wood. The materials came from homes that used to be on the property that we had demolished. We didn't want all of those materials to go to waste, so we learned how to refinish them and turn them into cabinetry. We built the kitchen with our own hands."

"Impressive," Vincent added.

"It's quite rewarding to live a life where we don't waste or consume so much there won't be anything left for future generations."

He walked over to a refrigerator and pulled out a pitcher of iced tea. He retrieved glasses from a cupboard, filled them, replaced the pitcher in the refrigerator, and handed us our beverages. "Enjoy. As you can see, we don't have any plastic materials here. This is all glass—recycled glass. But to be honest with you, we purchase them because we don't have the facility here to recycle glass. Maybe one day," he said with a chuckle.

He grabbed his glass of iced tea from the counter and said, "So, you came all the way out here from the Bay Area to talk to me. I'm an open book. What would you like to know?"

Vincent handed him the photo of Katie. "We're looking for a friend of ours named Katie Kimble. Her parents asked us to find her. They haven't heard from her in over two years, and they're afraid something bad has happened. You were dating Katie at the time she disappeared."

His head bowed forward and then returned upright, as if deep in thought. "Yes, Katie, such a spitfire. So much wonderful energy, not to mention an artist. She was really lovely."

"Do you know where Katie is?" I asked.

"I'm afraid not. We dated two years ago, and I thought we were happy. Then one day, she was just gone. I assumed she decided she didn't want to move in with me after all. I'd offered her a wonderful life, but she wouldn't have it, and I assumed she'd moved back with her parents. Is that not the case?"

"Afraid not. They haven't heard from her, and she hasn't been on social media in two years."

He furrowed his brow. "Now that is alarming. Well, if I run into anybody who might know where she is, I'll explain you're looking for her."

"That would be appreciated."

"Of course. How is the iced tea?"

The lemon was tart, and the tea was brewed perfectly. "It's great."

Vincent said, "It's the best iced tea I've ever had."

That obviously pleased Atlas. "Do you have any other questions for me? Or would you like to see more of the property? I enjoy giving tours, and it's so rare I get to do this."

"Sure, when in Rome." I raised my glass.

Atlas led us outdoors. There were more commune members around, and he waved to them with a grin. They all looked happy and well nourished. There didn't appear to be anything suspicious going on. I had been sure they were hiding something, but maybe I was wrong. It wouldn't be the first time.

As Atlas described the homes and how his community built them, we reached a section with multiple plants reeking of marijuana. "Oh, dear, we're not really supposed to be growing these here."

"Not to worry. We're not the police."

"Oh, good. You know, I really feel like some herbs can help open the mind, make you really feel life. At the compound, we don't consume alcohol, but we partake in other recreational activities. It helps us with our journey."

Their journey? Were they going somewhere? "When you say 'journey,' what do you mean?"

"Just the journey of life. I'm not one of those nut jobs who believes we're going in a spaceship up to the heavens. This is not a cult, Martina," he said playfully.

"Everybody seems happy and well fed."

"Of course, as they should be. We're all vegetarians. We pretty much only eat what we grow, except for a few supplies. We buy our rice and our beans. It's just easier that way. It takes up a lot of space, and we don't want to encroach on the natural beauty of the property by planting such a large number of crops."

Was it the marijuana they were hiding? Was that the reason for the privacy and the gate? Perhaps they were afraid of thieves as opposed to law enforcement.

We finished our tour, and within moments, a woman with dark hair and big doe eyes approached us. "I can take these for you." She pointed at our glasses.

"Thank you so much," I said, handing over my empty cup.

"Good to see you, Soleil," Atlas said to the woman as she hurried away. This was no ordinary community; I was guessing they had a leader, and Atlas was it.

"So, what is your story? Where did you grow up?" Vincent asked.

Atlas said, "I grew up on the East Coast. I came out to California for school. I went to college for a year, but I realized it wasn't for me. I had this idea after visiting a farm. You know, one of those places where you pick your own strawberries and your own apples. I wondered what it would be like to live on a farm, to only consume things you grow. After my parents passed and left me some money, I bought this property and started building. I would go back and forth between here and the Bay Area, meeting people who seemed to want the same kind of life, to forgo technology and the modern distractions. Ten years later, here we are."

"Incredible," I mused.

"It's never too late to make a change," Atlas added.

Indeed. It seemed like the only constant was change. "We appreciate you showing us around."

"Anytime. And, you know, our compound is not closed. If you ever feel that maybe this is the life for you, newcomers are always welcome. Both of you seem very nice, very relaxed," Atlas remarked.

"Yes, this is the first time I've ever seen anything like this. It's awesome," Vincent commented.

"It can be quite a shock to the senses to see something like this for the first time. Anytime you want to come, even just for a visit, or for a week or a month, you're welcome. The only thing we ask is that you help each other and yourself. We're a community, so we don't have just one person who helps grow and harvest the vegetables. It's everybody's responsibility to maintain our community," Atlas explained.

"That's so cool," Vincent said.

"It is absolutely cool. If you don't have any other questions, Sage will lead you back out."

"Appreciate it," I replied.

Instead of a handshake, he gave us a hug as we said goodbye. He told us to be well and go in peace.

Was it all for real? Had Katie really never been there? And did she run off without a word? If she had, why did he let her go so easily?

He said he'd assumed she went back to her parents and had changed her mind about moving in with him. But if they were so in love, wouldn't he have fought for her or tried to change her mind to come back to him? Or, at the very least, ensured she was safe? It sounded like Katie had told him, "I don't want this," and he never heard from her again and never questioned it.

Back at the quirky coffee shop overlooking the river, I met

up with the security team. They said they didn't see anything out of the ordinary other than it was obvious someone was watching for visitors, but they couldn't see much else. Vincent said, "Perhaps this is a dead end?"

That wasn't what my gut was saying. There was something off, but I couldn't put my finger on it. "Maybe. When we get back to the office tomorrow, let's dig into his background a little more."

"You got it, boss."

What would we find out about Jackson Galen?

12

___

MARTINA

Seated across from Daphne, Katie's last known best friend, I thanked her for meeting with me. With Vincent hard at work doing research on Atlas, also known as Jackson Galen, I took the interview alone. Daphne would likely be more comfortable with a female interviewer anyhow; she was young and might have been intimidated by two people questioning her.

"Sure, I've been worried about Katie," Daphne admitted.

"Why?"

"It's not really like her to just disappear. She always returned my texts and calls."

"Did you ever meet Atlas, her boyfriend?"

"Yeah, he was nice and good-looking, and she really liked him, and he seemed to really like her."

"Did anything seem strange about him? Did he treat her well?"

She shrugged. "He was older, like ten years older. That was a little strange, but he was just... he's got this presence about him. He was really nice and attentive. I think that's what Katie needed."

"When did you become worried about Katie?"

"Well, she told me she was moving with Atlas to his farm, but I tried her cell phone so many times, and she never answered. I thought that was strange."

If Katie had gone to the compound with Atlas and they didn't use any electronic goods, it would explain why she hadn't answered her phone. Maybe Katie didn't realize she would have to give up communication with her friends and family. Had Atlas made her choose between him and her old life? But Atlas told us people could come and go as they pleased. It didn't add up. "How long after she moved with Atlas did you try to contact her?"

"It was about a week later. I wanted to know how she was. I was thinking about coming to visit."

"Do you know where Atlas's farm was located?"

"Chico," she said. "At least, that's what she said."

His compound wasn't in Chico at all. Why had he lied to Katie's friend and her parents?

"What was Katie like when she was dating Atlas?"

"She was happy. She really was. I was happy for her."

"How long were they dating before she moved in with him?"

"Just a few months, but they hit it off so fast."

Fast love. Red flag. "Do you remember how they met?"

"He came into the coffee shop she was working at."

"Did she say what he ordered at the coffee shop?"

"That's funny. She did. She said it sparked their conversation about how tea was better for you than coffee. He ordered a green tea."

That tracked with his lifestyle: tea as opposed to cow's milk or a cheese and turkey sandwich. "What was Katie like before she met Atlas?"

"She was a free spirit, so when she met Atlas, it all made sense. Katie loved art, and she was so tired of her parents' expectations to go to college, get a respectable job, make money, pay for things… She didn't want any of that. She wanted a simpler life and to live in peace."

"Were there any problems at home other than her parents' expectations?"

Daphne seemed to shrink into herself. "She didn't get along with her father. He was really controlling, and she wanted to get away from him."

"Did he ever hurt Katie?"

"Not sexually," she said swiftly. "More like if she didn't have good enough grades, he'd smack her across the face. He did the same with her mom. He was physically abusive. It was never so bad she had broken bones or had to go to the hospital, but he would smack her around, push her, hold her up against the wall. She hated him."

It made sense why Katie would run away from home and not look back. But it didn't explain why she wouldn't talk to her friend Daphne. "Everything between you and Katie was okay before she left? There wasn't a falling out?"

Daphne's face softened and sadness filled her eyes. "No, we hugged, and I told her I couldn't wait for her to move to the farm and have the life she always wanted. Everything was great between us."

That was the part that didn't make sense. It was one thing for a young adult to leave home, but not calling her best friend was a different story. "Thank you for speaking with me today. If you think of anything else, or hear from Katie, call me."

She agreed.

As I left her apartment, I wondered what had happened to Katie. If she wasn't with Atlas, I worried about the alternative.

BACK ON THE ROAD, my phone buzzed. Using my new hands-free phone system, I answered, "Hello?"

"Martina, it's me, Zara."

"Is everything okay?" Zara was my sponsee. She'd been sober for eight days and was having a hard time with it.

"I just had a fight with my boyfriend, and I just really want to drink."

"Can you think of something else that you could do?"

"I called you."

"Do you want me to meet you? I can meet you at a coffee shop or come by your house. We can talk about this. You're not alone."

"Thank you, Martina. I'd like that. If you're not too busy."

I glanced at the clock on the dashboard. "I can meet you in half an hour."

"Thank you."

I made a U-turn at the next light and headed toward Zara's apartment and then called Vincent.

"Hey, boss. What's up?"

"I just came from Daphne, Katie's best friend's apartment. I will be out of the office a little longer, but I wanted to give you an update. Daphne told me that Katie's dad was abusive physically, so it made sense that she ran off and didn't call them. But Daphne said her and Katie's relationship was good, and she was surprised when she didn't hear from Katie. Daphne called her several times after she supposedly moved to a farm in Chico with Atlas."

"Atlas is a liar. We knew that, right? But I may have found something even more interesting."

We knew Atlas and Katie told her parents they were going to Chico, but a white lie to the parents was one thing. A lie to her best friend was a whole different story. "What did you find?"

"Well, you got me thinking the other day. I just looked up birth records for Jackson Galen, and guess what I found?"

"What?"

"Jackson Galen was born on the East Coast, but you know what else happened to Jackson Galen? He died six weeks later. Atlas is not Jackson Galen."

Well, then, who was he? If Atlas wasn't Jackson Galen, that meant he used a dead infant's information to build a new identity. Why? Who was Atlas, and more importantly, what or whom was he hiding from?

13

HIRSCH

Broken up over the latest news, I knew if we didn't stop the Sunny D dealers soon, we'd have more deaths on our hands. Jayda and Ross stepped into my office, and I leaned forward. "How did it go?" The team had spent the night following Ashworth Dante, who we suspected of supplying Zander Jenkins with the Sunny D we caught him selling.

Jayda crossed her arms. "We followed Ashworth back to his apartment, but he hasn't left the property. Zander's in custody. We want to question him, but we think we need eyes on Ashworth because there's no way he's making those drugs in his apartment."

Agreed. "Like I said, you've got unlimited OT all week. If you need backup, we can recruit the narcotics team. Let's keep Ashworth in our sights until we learn where the supply is coming from."

"I'm in," Ross declared.

Jayda added, "I'm in too. We gotta get these guys off the streets. Did you hear?"

"I did, two more. If we need more OT, more boots on the

ground, I'll get the sheriff to find more money. This is becoming a public health crisis. We need to end this fast."

Ross gave me a glance, as if he was implying something, but I was unsure what.

He tapped the side of his head, as if he had a bright idea. "You know, we've had tough cases in the past. We solved them after we brought in outside help."

I knew what kind of outside help he was referring to. And there wasn't much I wouldn't give to have Martina and Vincent back on the team helping us solve cases, especially one like Sunny D, where the longer it took us to find the suppliers, the more lives were lost. "I hear you. I'll talk to the sheriff. Any word from Rosemary?"

"She's still digging. She's working on the warehouse angle because they're likely manufacturing somewhere large enough for the required equipment. I think our best bet is to stay on Ashworth or try to get Zander to break. We were thinking you might want to join us. Maybe scare him into talking. He's an eighteen-year-old punk, never did hard time, just a few stints in juvie. Want to come with us?"

It had been a long time since I'd interrogated a suspect. Would I be rusty? "I'm in."

Jayda and Ross led the way to interrogation room one. Inside sat a skinny kid with shaggy hair and a sweatshirt three sizes too big. I steadied myself against the wall while Ross grabbed the chair in front of him and sat, staring at the suspect. Ross was a big guy. The tactic would intimidate *most* people. Jayda leaned against the table, her gaze fixed on Zander. Ross began, "Do you know why you're here, Zander?"

"I'm innocent, I swear. I didn't do it."

It was an act of control for me to not roll my eyes. The kid was naïve; you'd think he'd be a little smarter, having been in the system.

"That's interesting you say that because we've got these pictures telling us a different story."

The boy's eyes grew wide, filled with fear—as they should. This kid was looking at murder charges.

Jayda laid out a set of photographs taken two nights earlier. With each slap on the table, she described the images. "This first one here, you might recognize. Now check this next photo. You're handing something to this person, then in return, he hands you some cash."

"That's my friend. I was just saying hi, you know. He owed me money from the day before. We went to dinner, and I paid."

Jayda tsk tsked, showing her disappointment. "In this photo, if I can divert your attention over here, this is the person you say is your 'friend.' Can you see what they're holding in their hand?"

Zander sank into himself. "Looks like a bag of something."

"Yep, it is. Do you know what it is?"

"No," he stammered.

I stepped forward and peeked down at one photo. "Jayda, didn't our techs test that bag and find something interesting?" I asked, feigning ignorance.

Jayda stared at Zander. "We did. That's right, Zander, we sent that baggie to our lab, and we tested it against your fingerprints, and you know what they found out? They're yours. So, we actually can prove you were in possession of that item. Plus, we have the testimony of a scared kid saying you sold it to them. That's not all. Do you know what we found inside the bag? The kids on the street are calling it, Sunny D. It's LSD laced with a lethal dose of fentanyl. And you want to know what else, Zander? These drugs have killed *five* people."

Seeing Jayda's anger, Ross stood up and played the good cop, trying to calm her. I'd seen their act before; it was pretty good.

With the path to Zander clear, I stared right at him and said, "Zander, my name is Sergeant Hirsch. What my detectives haven't told you yet is that because we can prove you sold these drugs to people who later died, that puts you on the hook for first-degree murder. Many people don't realize if a person is killed during a felony act or because of it, like drug dealing, that bumps the charge to first-degree. We're talking about life in prison, if not the death penalty. So, you can pretend to not know anything and risk going to jail for the rest of your life, or you can tell us who gave you the drugs to sell. Because we know you're not the big fish; we know that you're just a kid caught up in something heavy. If you were my son, I'd recommend you tell us the truth because then you'd give yourself half a chance at a normal life."

With far less confidence, he said, "Can I really get murder charges?"

"Absolutely. These drugs are deadly. Five people have died. Five people your age. Young people just trying to have fun. Your supplier messed up the formula, and they're killing people, and they're putting you right in the spotlight, making it look like it's all your fault, Zander. Unless you can tell us who else is involved, who's making these deadly party favors, who's killing these people, it's all going to come down on you. If you talk to us, we can help you. If not, that's it for you."

He sat back and studied the three of us. "I'll talk. Off the record."

Ross, Jayda, and I exchanged a look. I said, "Okay."

"I don't know much."

I knew none of this could be used in a court of law, but that wasn't my concern. I wanted to know who was behind the drugs. "How do you know Ashworth?"

"You mean Ash?" he asked, confused.

"Yeah, Ash."

"I met him through my girlfriend. She's a preppy type, living in the suburbs. He's a friend of one of her friends' boyfriends. He asked me if I wanted to make some easy cash. Ash said the stuff sells itself and I wouldn't have to go to downtown Oakland or somewhere dangerous to sell it. All I had to do was hang out in Berkeley by the campus and by the local community colleges. The college kids beg for it. Easy money."

"Where does Ash get the drugs from?" I asked.

"I don't know. I didn't ask."

"How often does he replenish your supply?"

"Every night."

"Do you know how often he picks up his supply?"

"I don't know. I swear."

With a respectful nod, I said, "Thanks for talking with us, Zander. We appreciate your honesty. We'll help you through this as long as you're truthful with us. Do that, and I'll make sure you don't get hard time."

With his cooperation, he'd likely get probation. It was a good sign he'd been smart enough to not ask questions about the organization. That gave me hope he could turn his life around.

"Thank you," he replied softly.

Staring down at the kid, I said, "When you get past this, you can turn your life around. Go back to school. Go to college. This is a dangerous business, not something you want to stick with."

"Who's going to pay for me to go to college? There ain't nobody caring about me. Helping me."

"Not true. I care. There are a lot of programs for people who can't afford college. They'll even give you a stipend to live on while you're going to junior college. You can make something of yourself."

The look in his eyes was something I didn't think I'd ever forget. It was as though it was the first time anyone even pretended to act like they cared about him. "I'm serious. I'll make a few calls and get you that information. There is another way. Did they read you your rights?"

He nodded.

"Do you want something?" I asked, trying to hint he needed to ask for a lawyer.

"I want a lawyer."

After a wink and nod, I said, "We'll call over now. Take care of yourself."

He mumbled, "Thanks."

Out in the hall, I told Jayda and Ross, "My guess is that's all he knows."

"Agreed. You really gonna get him some info?" Jayda asked.

"He's an eighteen-year-old kid. It's obvious nobody's taken a chance on him, nobody has told him there's another way, that there's funding to pay for him to live and go to school, to choose a different path. But I told him. Did you see the look on his face? We don't want more drug dealers on the corner. One day, he's a drug dealer, the next, he moves on to worse just to survive. I can take five minutes out of my day to make sure he's got a social worker who will help him and give him a chance to get out."

"That's deep, boss," Ross said.

"That's life. That's probably all he'll give us. Let's do round-the-clock surveillance on Ashworth to find out where he's getting the drugs."

"Yes, sir," Jayda said with a smile.

Back in my office, I looked up the information for a social worker to get in contact with Zander. In this job, I didn't want to just catch criminals; I wanted people to stop being criminals. Zander was young. He still had a chance to get out of that life. If he got out, it might save his life and others' too. How much better could this world be if we all spent just five minutes to help a stranger?

14

FERN

With my bare hands, I dug a hole and carefully placed the tomato plant inside, then filled it in with loose soil. I hoped keeping busy would keep my mind off things, or at least keep me calm. I needed to get out of there, to escape without Atlas knowing. If he knew I wanted to leave, he wouldn't be pleased, and I wasn't sure I'd make it out alive.

I'd been beating myself up about not seeing the signs earlier —his controlling behavior, the violence. How, when we first met, he said it was fate, that he loved me after only a week. That should've been my first red flag. He called me constantly, texted me, and said he wanted to be with me every minute. I should've known it was too good to be true.

I'd been a fool to agree to move with him after only a few months. As soon as he had me away from my old life, he took everything away, and I didn't even see it until it was gone. As long as I agreed with everything he wanted, peace remained. But if I ever went against him, or if anyone ever went against him, it ended badly. Yet, I still wished he was who I thought he was. I really did. But now, knowing the truth, I was terrified and needed to get out.

As I moved over to plant another tomato, I noticed my hands shaking. I needed to stop thinking about this, especially in public. Nobody could know what I was feeling, what I was planning.

Soleil knelt down across from me. "Hi, Fern, how's it going?"

"Great. I just have a few more tomato plants, and then I might take a break. Are you enjoying the community?"

"Oh, very much," she replied, smiling. "It's so great here, isn't it?"

"It really is."

Soleil had been in the community for only a few months. She hadn't gotten on Atlas's bad side yet. If she had, she wouldn't be here anymore. I wondered if one day Atlas would make Soleil take care of someone like he made me. It was strange to love somebody that you also feared. Why couldn't he just be who he pretended to be? Because it was all *fake*. Wasn't it?

"Would you like to join me for lunch?" Soleil asked.

"After I plant these, absolutely."

Most members of the community were kind and peaceful creatures, just like Atlas had promised us. Soleil hadn't been tainted by the dark side of him, the side he hid from most people. Once he showed it, it couldn't be forgotten. Why had I let him lead me down this path? The things that I had done—I never would've thought I'd sink so low or do so many terrible things. I had killed a woman, Opal, and I didn't even know her real name.

As Soleil dug another hole, she asked, "What should we have for lunch?"

"How about a salad with that new vinaigrette Cloud made the other day. It's amazing, isn't it?"

"Oh, yes," she replied. "Sounds incredible. I can't wait. I'm famished."

"And there's still some peanut butter cookies left."

"Okay, now my mouth is watering."

I liked Soleil; she was pure; she was sweet. I wondered how long it would be before Atlas took her to his dark side, made her do what he wanted her to do. She probably wouldn't even fight him. She would trust she was doing it for the greater good, to help the community. Was that how he had convinced me to do what I had done?

After lunch, I hurried to my room, explaining to Soleil I was going to wash up before Atlas and I left for some errands. But really, my nerves were getting the better of me, and I knew I was going to break down at any moment.

Inside Atlas and my room, I thought about all the things I had done. What a fool I'd been. I was now a criminal, and my only option was to be on the run, not only from Atlas, but from the police, too. If I escaped, where would I go? Who would even take me in? I wasn't who I was before. Sometimes, I didn't remember who I was, other than a total idiot.

As my mind raced, I broke down and cried. I was so ashamed of myself, of the things I'd done. I tried to make the tears stop, tried to calm myself by breathing deeply like we did in yoga every morning, but it didn't help. It just made me cry more. I couldn't let Atlas see me like this; he would know something was wrong.

The door creaked open, and there he stood. His eyes met mine, and he quickly shut the door behind him. "What's wrong?" he asked.

"Nothing," I lied. "I'm just being emotional today, just happy with all of our blessings." That was the best I could come up with. I needed to shake off the real reason I was crying or come up with a better story.

"You don't have to worry. We're in the clear."

"I know. I'm just being emotional. I'm fine, I promise."

He knelt down in front of me and said, "Is this about what happened? Do you feel guilty? Don't feel guilty. She would've ruined all of us."

"How many others are there?" I asked, with tears still in my eyes.

His eyes went dark. I didn't like it when his eyes went dark. "You don't need to worry about that," he replied curtly. He stood up and stepped back, looking me up and down. My body trembled as he assessed me. "Can I trust you, Fern?"

"Of course. I'm just being emotional. Hormones. I'll be fine."

"I'm going alone today. You'll stay here."

"But I always go with you," I said, surprised and disappointed. It was the perk of being his chosen one. Supposedly, I was his partner, but in reality, I was more like his best servant. Why had I ever thought otherwise? More frightening, was he planning to replace me? If he replaced me, where would I go? To another home on the property, or would he get rid of me completely?

"Not today," he said firmly. "Don't leave this room until I return. I can't have you upsetting the others."

Fear gripped my soul. "But you'll be gone for hours. What if I get hungry?"

"You will not leave this room until I return. If you do, I will know, and there will be consequences." With that, he turned and left.

He had put me in a prison. The only bars were his words, yet they were as strong as steel. What was I going to do?

15

MARTINA

Nestled in the driveway of what appeared to be an empty vacation home down the hill from Atlas's compound, we waited. We were uncertain of the duration of our stakeout, whether it would be an hour, fifteen minutes, or if it would extend into the night. Hopefully, it wouldn't take that long. The car was quiet and stuffy, and I would rather be outside, enjoying the cool breeze coming off the ocean. It was a gorgeous, sunny day, and I could think of about ten different ways to spend my time that were far better than sitting in a car with Vincent. No offense to Vincent, but hiking sounded nice, or maybe a workout at the gym—really, anything other than a stakeout. Action was much preferred to sitting and waiting. That said, Vincent wasn't the worst company.

Suddenly, Vincent pulled the cell phone up to his ear. "Hello," he said, breaking the silence. Did Steve and Otto have an update? Had we missed Atlas leaving his property? He glanced at me and said okay before ending the call. "That was Steve. While at the coffee shop, they heard some locals talking about the 'hippies'—presumably Atlas and his pals living on the commune. Apparently, they're not very popular."

"They say why?"

"Said they don't come around much, only when they need gas, or occasionally to use the phone."

We knew Atlas had an active cell phone, so the locals must be referring to other members of the community. Did Atlas lie to his community about his cell phone usage? What else had Atlas lied about, and why? He'd lied to Daphne, Katie's best friend, about where he lived and even had a completely fake identity, a sophisticated one. It made me wonder who we were really dealing with. Was he truly some peace-out hippie getting high and enjoying Mother Nature? If that were true, why the fake identity? And then I realized, maybe it was more than that. Maybe he was not a criminal at all, maybe he was in witness protection.

"Are they rude to the locals?"

"No, they said they're strange and don't trust them," Vincent explained. "They said usually this is a place where people come to retire or go for a getaway, not to have some weird hippie commune. They're all pretty sure they just sit around doing drugs. One neighbor said they smell marijuana smoke constantly."

It wasn't exactly a smoking gun. "They could be worse neighbors, right?" I suggested with a hint of humor.

"True," Vincent agreed. "But they also theorize the group is a cult because there's something's off about them."

What something? I could understand their sentiments, and I tried to figure out exactly what was off about the commune, too. There was definitely something amiss, but was it my own preconceived notions that people should live as part of the greater society, partaking in technology, arts, and community, as opposed to hiding away and creating their own? Was it a simple case of people not trusting people who were different from them?

"Maybe so," I mused. "Maybe they're just different and so people think there's something wrong with that."

"True," Vincent agreed. "But it all seems a little *too* perfect."

I knew what he meant. We couldn't find a single flaw in their commune. Everyone was friendly and welcoming. Why was I still suspicious? Was it because I knew human nature wouldn't allow that kind of harmony? It was pretty obvious Atlas was their leader, and if it was a true commune, there wouldn't be an actual leader, would there?

"Agreed," I echoed. "Did the locals say anything about any run-ins with them, any kind of trouble?"

"No. Just that everybody wishes they were gone. They're too strange for them, as if they're trying to relive the sixties."

Maybe they were, but that wasn't exactly illegal. Staring out the windshield, I saw no movement except for birds fluttering between the treetops.

"It's pretty cool here, right?" Vincent asked.

"It is. Makes you wonder if their way of life is really all that strange."

"True," Vincent responded. "But if I were a betting person, I'd bet there's something really wrong there."

"Why?"

"I just get a feeling, Martina. Atlas's fake identity, lying about where his farm is to Katie's friend and parents, how quickly they appear when you drive up to the compound. Something is definitely off there, and the show they put on for us, I think it was just that—a show."

Vincent had good instincts. He always had. It was why I wasn't surprised he'd inquired about becoming a private investigator when the cold case squad disbanded. He was a natural fit, and although only on the job for five years as a private investigator, he was one of our best. You can't really teach instincts, and Vincent had them.

The sound of an engine grabbed my attention as well as Vincent's. Peering out the windshield, we spotted a blue SUV coming down the hill. Behind the wheel was a single man with long sandy hair and a bushy beard. It was Atlas.

We both ducked down, and Vincent called Steve. "Just spotted a blue SUV. He's moving your way."

We remained in place, and I stared at my watch, waiting a full ninety seconds before turning on the engine. We didn't want him to know we were watching his community, as they called it. The timer went off, and I started the car.

"Let's find out where he goes," I voiced out. Where would Atlas lead us? Would it be to a Costco or a local grocery to get supplies like he'd sworn he'd done just a few days earlier? Or would we learn what Atlas was really up to?

16

———

MARTINA

ADRENALINE PUMPING, I kept a wide distance from the blue SUV. Steve and Otto followed close after pulling out of the coffee shop parking lot. Vincent took calls and updates from Steve and Otto about Atlas's location as I focused on the winding road and steep cliffs ahead. We continued for about twenty minutes until we hit Bodega Bay, a crowded little town filled with tourists and crab shacks.

Vincent said, "Otto says they're ahead about half a mile and it's much more crowded. They're only a few cars behind Atlas."

"Good."

"What was that movie filmed in Bodega Bay?"

"*The Birds*, by Hitchcock," I recalled. "That movie creeped me out. I've been here a few times though. It has a kind of ominous feeling, but that's probably just because I watched the movie too many times when I was younger."

The once scene of a classic horror movie was now popularized by tourists happily eating taffy along the coast and staring out at the sparkling blue water as children played in the surf.

An incoming call from Otto interrupted our conversation.

"I'll put it on speaker," Vincent announced. He clicked the button. "Hi, Otto, we have you on speaker."

"Atlas is headed south on CA-1 and just turned left onto Bodega Highway," he reported.

"Did you notice anything out of the ordinary? Is he on a cell phone?"

"Nope, just driving around like a happy little camper," Otto replied.

"Thanks, Otto," Vincent said as he ended the call. "You know, this is exciting for the first, like, five minutes, but then it's just constant driving."

"Am I boring you, Vincent?"

"Oh, no, you're top-notch entertainment. I'm just eager to learn more about Atlas," he joked back.

Twenty minutes later, another call came in. "We're heading east on CA-12 toward Santa Rosa," Otto updated us.

"Thanks."

Vincent ended the call and said, "Excellent. I'll be happy to be off these windy roads. You know, I was telling Amanda about Jenner, that eclectic coffee spot, and the commune."

"Do you typically talk about cases with Amanda?"

"No, I was just telling her about their way of life and the scenery. You know, to see if it was something she might be interested in for our future, when we're older," he explained.

Vincent wasn't a young pup anymore, but he wasn't exactly seasoned, either.

"Oh? Thinking about your future with Amanda?" I asked, interested. As boring as stakeouts were, when you had a partner, you learned a lot about each other. Vincent and Amanda had been together for at least six years, and I knew they were serious, but I didn't know he'd been contemplating their future.

"Yeah, my 30th birthday is coming up, and it makes me think about the kind of life I want to have. Do I want kids, a wife, a house with a white picket fence and little yellow flowers outside?" he pondered.

Interesting. "And what conclusion did you come to?"

"Well, I'm not sure..."

His train of thought appeared to have drifted, and I wondered if he didn't really want to talk about it.

As I headed onto CA-12, I said, "Well, a family and children are a blessing if that's what you want. Thirty isn't very old. You have time to decide. We're never too old to make changes. Take my mom as an example."

"Your mom is pretty cool."

I had to agree. We'd reconnected eight years ago after a rocky start. We were both recovering alcoholics; I was eight years sober, she was nine. She and I were examples of people who could change for the better. It had taken some time, but I'd let go of the resentment against the childhood I'd had, living in a home with an alcoholic mother and an absent father. It didn't serve me to keep all that bottled up.

My intuition told me Vincent was about to continue speaking about Amanda and his future when the phone buzzed again. He answered on speaker. "What's up?"

"Our guy's getting off on Santa Rosa Avenue."

"All right, we'll catch up."

We were only about a mile behind Steve and Otto, and I wondered if we needed another backup team. I didn't know where Atlas was going or if he was meeting with anyone. Heart racing, knowing we were close to finding the truth, Vincent and I remained quiet as we exited the highway.

"Where are you now, Steve?" Vincent asked.

"Turning right on Yolanda Avenue. Looks residential. Lots of warehouses."

"All right," Vincent said as I stepped on the gas, breaking the speed limit just a tad. "Okay, we see you now."

"He's parked outside a warehouse. The address is 3024. Big blue building. We're going to park and keep an eye out," Steve informed us.

"Good," Vincent acknowledged.

We eased our way down the street, sailed past Steve and Otto's black sedan, and parked around the corner where we were less conspicuous but still had a sightline on the warehouse.

With Steve still on the line, he reported, "We have our cameras out. Our pal's on the move. He's talking on a cell phone and walking toward the entrance of the building."

Atlas used his cell phone, and it was a secret from his community members. But why? Why keep such a secret from the others? Was he, perhaps, a false prophet?

Eyes fixed on the building and its surroundings, we waited for something to happen.

Thirty minutes later, the adrenaline began to fade, and I couldn't help but wonder what was going on inside. Who was Atlas meeting with? "Who's that guy?" Vincent suddenly asked. "Steve, do you see that? The guy in the blue blazer and khaki pants?"

"Yeah, I've got photos. He doesn't appear to have anything in his hands," Steve replied over the speaker.

"Maybe it's a men's club like the Freemasons," I pondered aloud, seeking input from anyone on the call.

"I don't know, but they've definitely grabbed my attention," Vincent responded, glancing at me. "It's getting late."

"We can stay on if you need us to, Martina," Steve offered.

It was Friday night, and I didn't have plans, but Barney was at home by himself. I could ask my mom to go by and play with him, so he'd know the entire Monroe family hadn't abandoned him.

"Wait, here's our guy," Steve alerted us over the speaker.

Atlas headed back to his SUV. What had he been doing

inside the building for an hour and a half, and then to stroll out empty-handed?

"Do you want to tail him, or should we?" Otto asked.

"Go ahead and follow him," I suggested. "Keep us updated. Let us know the direction he goes. We'll stay back for a bit."

"You got it, boss," Steve affirmed as the call ended.

I glanced over at Vincent. "Got plans tonight?"

"I could cancel them," he said, albeit reluctantly.

Not necessary. Steve and Otto could handle it. "We can go back, otherwise traffic will be a nightmare."

"You're the boss," he reminded me.

"When we get back to the office, we need to do more digging. I want to get inside that warehouse and see what goes on in there, but we should learn more before storming in." Going in blind was both stupid and dangerous.

Vincent agreed. "I can pull records, see who owns the building. Maybe it's rented out. Maybe it has a business registered to it."

It was a smart approach, but I'd be lying if I didn't say my skin was itching to get inside and find out what Atlas was doing at a random warehouse in Santa Rosa. As we drove away, I thought, *Atlas, what are you up to?*

17

______

FERN

Two days had passed since I'd seen or heard from Atlas. My theory that his anger would burn off and he would return after running errands was debunked on the first day. The first clue was the knock on the door. Atlas didn't knock. Why would he? On the other side of the door was Huck, my least favorite member of our community. He brought me food and told me Atlas asked him to keep an eye on me and make sure I didn't leave. The look in his eyes told me he was prepared to do anything to keep me there. Huck was not a regular in the community; he came from time to time to monitor things. I didn't know where he lived or what his story was, but the tattoos on his arm and around his neck told me enough.

At first, I had naively thought Huck had turned over a new leaf, that he was different. But he wasn't. There was a darkness in him, but he didn't fight it; he reveled in it. The way he looked me up and down, before licking his lips, was disgusting. Why did Atlas let him stick around? He clearly wasn't one of us.

With a lot of solo time to think, I realized I had to stop blaming Atlas or Huck or anybody else for my circumstances. It was my naivety that trapped me in a place I used to call home.

When I was young, in my early teens, I'd envisioned what my life would look like. I would go to art school, live in an apartment in a big city, maybe Madrid or Barcelona, and study the greats, visit art galleries and museums daily. I would learn about culture and gain valuable experience. Naïve then and naïve now.

The worst part of all this was I had believed everything Atlas said because I wanted to. I loved the idea of a place where we could shake off all the trappings of society and just exist, create art, appreciate life and nature. But how quickly my perspective had shifted. I thought of Huck with his beefy arms and his evil glares. I was no different from him. Was I?

Who knows, maybe he was once like me. He likely never envisioned this would be how his life turned out, keeping some young woman captive because her criminal boyfriend asked him to. Surely no little kid says they want to grow up to be a thug. Or who knows, maybe they do.

With all this time to myself, I knew the only way out was to flee.

When there was a knock on the door, I knew he was back. At least he didn't just barge in; he was being polite. Likely that was just for show, so nobody would question why he'd be storming into my cabin.

I opened the door and smiled. "Well, hello, Huck. How are you today?"

"Super. I brought you a lovely dinner: a nice garden salad with vinaigrette, some homemade rolls, and a side of rice and tofu."

At least Atlas was decent enough to feed me. He could've starved me. Maybe he really loved me, but he didn't know how to do it right. I couldn't believe I was still making excuses for him. For a second, I even thought he actually loved me. But then again, maybe this was how he showed love; he didn't immediately shoot me in the head because I disobeyed him and went against his teachings. He could have, but he hadn't.

I said, "Thank you so much."

"I'll set it down on the table for you."

What a gentleman. "Did Atlas say when he was coming back?" I asked, hoping for a hint about his plans.

He set down the tray, and the glasses rattled. "Didn't say. He said it might be a few days. Don't worry. He'll be back for you."

Back for me? Was he going somewhere? He wouldn't leave his community. For all his faults, Atlas loved the compound and the garden. I had never seen any red meat; he was a vegan like the rest of us. Then again, we weren't all one way or the other, were we? All villains have a softer side too, don't they?

When exactly had I turned into a villain? It seemed logical to point to the moment I pulled the trigger, but it wasn't. It was before that. I had been a villain for so long, my old self had shrunk away. But now, I wished I could remember her, bring her back, but I feared it was too late.

"I'm going to be leaving for the day. Is there anything else I can get you?" Huck asked nicely, likely following Atlas's orders or to keep up with appearances.

"No. Where are you going?" Was this my opportunity to run?

"Not to worry. Forrest is going to take care of you. He'll be checking in periodically to see if you need anything."

I was still a prisoner. At least Forrest wasn't like Huck. Forrest had started off pure, like so many who came to the community, but he turned and quickly embraced the darkness, just like I had.

As I watched the burly man leave, I questioned if I had anything left to lose. Maybe I should throw all caution to the wind and make a run for it. I knew the compound like the back of my hand. If I was quick and quiet, I could reach the main road.

And then what?

There wasn't anything for miles. And with utter darkness, traffic wouldn't see me. And if I tried to stand out, surely someone from the community would be looking and take me back. Was there no way out?

18

MARTINA

Seated across from my favorite ex-partner, my insides warmed as he doted on about Audrey. Hirsch and I did weekly lunches after our partnership had disbanded. We both agreed bouncing ideas off one another about each other's cases would be beneficial, and it gave us a chance to catch up. We obviously talked frequently, especially with Zoey being Audrey's favorite babysitter. But it still wasn't the same as actually working together. I was settled into my role, running Drakos Monroe Security & Investigations, but I missed my days at the CoCo County Sheriff, too. "I feel like I'm going to blink and Audrey will be sixteen, just like Zoey."

"I know that feeling. It feels like yesterday Zoey was five years old, leaving glitter all over our house. Not that she doesn't still make signs for the different sports teams she's taking part in or her student body election posters."

"So, what you're telling me is the glitter's never going away and I'll continue to sparkle even if I don't want to?"

I chuckled. "Yep." Glitter stuck to everything. Clothes and hair. *Forever.*

Sipping my iced tea, I asked, "Any interesting new cases?"

Hirsch wiped the corner of his mouth with a napkin. "Actually, yeah. We're in the middle of a big one. But we're not making as much progress as I'd like."

"Another serial killer?" I joked. Hirsch had always accused me of attracting serial killers just so we could solve the case.

"You're not too far off. In some ways, yes. Ross reminded me in the old days, we used to hire outside consultants to help us with tough cases like this one."

Was he serious? I wasn't sure, so I let him continue.

"This one has five deaths associated with it. A street drug. They're calling it Sunny D—LSD laced with fentanyl. Our only suspects are a low-level drug dealer and his supplier. The supplier hasn't been back for his resupply for several days. It feels like we're getting nowhere with the case."

Five murders? "Who's working it?"

"Couple of our guys from narcotics, and Jayda and Ross from the old squad."

"Sounds like it's in excellent hands."

"It is, but if we don't get info to crack the case soon, we may have to put together a task force. It's that big. We don't think the dealer is intentionally killing his customers. No customers, no money."

"Sounds like a biggie." Was I jealous?

"Exactly. My team ran out of their allotted overtime. I have to meet the sheriff later today to see how to handle the case. It's huge. I don't want kids to keep dying on the street because they tried to get some LSD for a fun Friday night. Not that I think they should be out taking LSD, but they shouldn't have to pay for it with their lives."

"Kids?"

"Pretty much. College-age, late teens, early twenties. We think if we can't stop the supplier, the body count will continue to rise."

It'd been ages since I'd had such a high-stakes case, and I admit I was envious. Not that the missing person investigation for Katie Kimble wasn't throwing us for a loop and keeping us on our toes. But I longed for the rush of saving the innocent, bringing in the bad guys, and locking them up forever.

"Sounds like a task force to me."

"That will be determined by the sheriff and what kind of budget he'll give us. We need to have a press release to warn the public to avoid LSD because it may contain a lethal dose of fentanyl. It might make it more difficult for us to find who is manufacturing the drugs, but it could prevent future deaths."

"Rock and a hard place."

Hirsch nodded.

"So, will we be seeing your face on the news tonight? I'll be sure to tune in."

He shrugged. "Probably. I'm going to propose to the sheriff we do it as soon as possible. We already have five dead, and I don't want any more."

"Do you have anybody in custody?"

"Just a low-level kid. He doesn't know much. He'll probably get off with probation. I've hooked him up with a social worker to get him into school. He's only eighteen. In and out of juvenile hall. He never had a chance. I'm hoping to turn that around."

I cocked my head, surprised by Hirsch's words. "Oh, yeah?"

"Yeah, I'm a big softy now. Besides putting away the bad guys, I'd like to reform a few, especially the young ones. You should have seen this kid. He didn't have a clue they had laced the drugs with fentanyl. It's not right his life gets ruined because of a group of greedy drug dealers."

"You think the system failed him?"

"I do. He had a few stints in juvie but never once got hooked up with a social worker who could help him get back into school and come onto the straight and narrow. There's not enough information given to at-risk kids. They need to understand there's a way."

Hirsch's attitude impressed me. He'd always been one of the best men I'd ever known, but I thought becoming a parent had definitely made him see things in a different light.

"Any ideas, outside of a task force, how to move forward in the Sunny D case?"

"I love your idea of reforming those you can. Trust me, one less bad guy and one more good guy is a win for me. But as for your case, if it were me, I'd start following anybody who is associated with the low-level drug dealer. Friends, associates, the supplier. I would keep my eyes on them."

"That's the plan... but the budget. Hence the meeting with the sheriff."

That was one thing we didn't have to deal with at Drakos Monroe. Our clients paid us when they could, and when they couldn't, we covered it. We had enough high-level operations to fund a budget to assist those who couldn't pay the full fees. That was a perk of being in private practice. Our mission wasn't so much to put away the bad guys as it was to find the missing, help the victims, and protect the innocent. The police took care of the rest.

"Enough about my woes. Anything interesting on your side, or are you mostly managing the firm?"

"Actually, I'm working on a case with Vincent."

"Yeah?" He took a bite of his chicken marsala.

"A missing person. She's been missing for two years, but it's unusual. She had a boyfriend when she disappeared. The parents thought he was too good to be true, too smooth, and maybe even controlling. So far, we've found the boyfriend, and he's lied about his identity and where he lived."

"Do you think he did something to the missing woman?"

"If he didn't, I think he knows where she is. It's strange

though. He lives on a commune up the coast. It's gorgeous actually. You might think 'Oh, peaceful people,' and that's what they tell us. But when we looked into his background, it's all fake. Initially, we looked him up and found he's a guy named Jackson Galen. But then, Vincent dug even further and realized Jackson Galen died at six weeks old."

Hirsch's blue eyes widened, and he set down his fork and finished chewing. "He's got a fake identity? A real one, like a sophisticated one."

"Exactly. Not something you get on the streets."

"That's definitely interesting. Just the two of you working it?"

"We have backup when we do surveillance. Something feels really off there, but I can't put my finger on it. Nothing is pointing us to what's going on with this guy. When we spoke to him, he said he hadn't seen the woman for two years either, and that she had been living with him, but she ran off saying it wasn't the life for her."

He smirked. "That doesn't sound likely."

"No, but the weird part is the people living in the community seem to be guarding it, too. During our tour the boyfriend graciously provided, we didn't see any weapons or military gear, but within seconds of pulling up to the property, they appeared at the gate to greet us. We've been there three times, and each time, they appear within seconds."

"They're definitely hiding something."

"That's what we think. We think the key is to stay on Atlas, the boyfriend."

"Let me ask you this," Hirsch began. "If I talk to the sheriff and we have to put together a task force, do you have anybody on your team who could help out?" There was a look in his eyes I knew very well.

"It would depend on the timing. Vincent and I are pretty

wrapped up in this missing person case, and it keeps getting stranger by the minute. But we have other staff who could help."

Despite his efforts, I could tell Hirsch was suppressing a smile. "Typical Martina case."

I shrugged. "What can I say? It's a gift."

We both looked into each other's eyes, and if I had to bet, I'd say we were thinking the same thing—we missed the old days. But we shouldn't forget the current days were a blessing, too. "I'll let you know if anything happens with the sheriff or if we need some of Drakos Monroe's services."

"We're always open for business."

"And there's something a little more sensitive I probably should warn you about."

That was unusual. "Yeah?"

"Jayda is bringing a friend to the barbecue on Saturday."

"Isn't she married?"

"She is. She's bringing a friend she thinks may be a good match with *somebody* who's not married."

I almost spit out my iced tea. "She's trying to set me up?"

Hirsch raised his hands up in the air in defense. "I had nothing to do with it. All I said was she could bring a friend to the barbecue."

It had been a long while since I'd been on a date. But I had to admit, I wouldn't mind meeting someone special. Not that Barney, my ten pounds of fluff, wasn't good company. He was loving, he was cuddly, and he never complained. Barney was always fully supportive of everything I did in my life, except for, of course, leaving the house. But a human partner? I wasn't against it. "Did she tell you anything about him?"

Hirsch's brows shot up. "You're interested?"

"I'm not against it."

"Well, you know, if you want a setup, Kim has some friends we could hook you up with."

The phrases 'setup' and 'hook you up' didn't sound as nice as 'meeting someone' did.

"Is it too much to think I could meet somebody organically, in my everyday life, and not be set up like some sad spinster?"

"You're *not* a sad spinster. You deserve to be happy, Martina, and I think when the right person comes along, you'll know it. Sounds like you may be ready to meet that someone."

"Thanks, Hirsch." We finished our meal and talked about how good it would be to see everybody at the barbecue on Saturday. We said our goodbyes, and I headed back to the office.

As I strolled through the lobby, I wondered if I'd be open to working on a special task force for the sheriff's department. It would depend on the case and if I had the time. As far as I was concerned, Katie Kimble was my number one priority. In my heart, I knew I'd like to work with Hirsch and the team again, but Katie would be my focus until we found her.

On the way to my office, Vincent approached, waving me down. "Got a minute?"

"Sure. What's up?"

"I spoke with the owner of the warehouse in Santa Rosa. Turns out, he rented it to a guy. A guy who said he's making soap."

"Soap?"

"Yeah, get this, the guy's name is Jeff Imogene. The building owner says it's a gentleman's agreement, so it won't show up on any records. Jeff Imogene has been renting the space for about a year."

"Are there any businesses registered to the property?"

"Nope."

"Don't businesses have to be registered if they're operating?"

"Usually."

"If it's not our guy, Atlas, may be an associate?"

"I'm not so sure that's the case. On a hunch, I asked him to describe Jeff. He says he's got long, sandy hair, a big beard. A hippie type."

"Atlas with yet another alias?"

"That's where my money's at."

What was Atlas doing with that warehouse? I'd bet my retirement it wasn't making soap. With that, we made plans to return to the warehouse for round-the-clock surveillance. We needed to get in, to see what was really going on. And more importantly, to learn what Atlas had done with Katie.

MARTINA

On my knees, I picked up the ball and threw it across the living room. Barney rushed after it, proud of himself. He chewed on it for a bit before scurrying back to me and dropping it on the floor so we could do it all over again. Taking his cue, I chucked the ball across the room just as Zoey walked into the living room.

"Hey, Mom, I'm leaving soon. Is Grandma coming over?"

"She is. She's going to stay with Barney. It'll be a late night for me; stakeout with Vincent."

"So cool, stakeouts and all that stuff," she said as she fluffed her hair. I still remembered her as a little girl covered in pink and sparkles. What stood before me was a young woman, nearly as tall as I was at 5'6" with long dark brown hair, bright blue eyes, and a perfect complexion. She was gorgeous, and it frightened me. "Oh, yeah? Are you thinking of going into law enforcement or into investigations?"

She bit her lower lip and hesitated. "It's super cool to think about, but I think I'd like to be a veterinarian or a pediatrician."

"I think you could do anything you put your mind to."

"Thanks, Mom."

"What are your plans tonight?"

"Well, I considered going to the library with Kaylie, but she has a date with her *boyfriend*." She said it as if it was an atrocity that Kaylie would ditch their study session for a boy.

"Sometimes things like that happen."

"Yeah, maybe I'll just come home after school and hang out with Grandma."

A pang of jealousy hit me. "She's going to stay over. I'll likely be out all night."

"Okay. Be safe, and always remember to be aware of your surroundings."

She'd always been a wiseacre, but her teenage years had proven she could push that even further. "You too."

"I always am," she said as she headed into the kitchen.

I envied Zoey's confidence.

A key in the door caused Barney to abandon his ball play and rush toward the front door, jumping at it and barking. As soon as the door opened, he quieted and jumped up at my mother's legs. "Oh, hello, Barney. I missed you, too."

He ran inside, and Mom followed. "Hi, dear. Oh, and there's my lovely granddaughter."

Zoey exited the kitchen and came up to my mother to give her a hug. I stood up and did the same. "Big stakeout tonight?"

"Yep. How's Ted?"

"Ted's good. He went fishing today."

Ted was definitely enjoying his retirement. "I saw on the news last night Hirsch caught himself a pretty big case. Drugs killing young people. Awful. Zoey, have you heard about this?"

"No worries. I'm not buying any LSD."

"You should warn your friends. This is serious. Hirsch says five people have died." Even if Zoey wasn't using drugs, I wasn't naïve enough to believe kids at her high school weren't.

"I know it's serious. Trust me, none of my friends are doing LSD," she said, as if it was a ridiculous notion.

I remembered being young and thinking I knew everything. As I got older, I'd realized how much I hadn't known. It terrified me how much I still didn't know that I would only realize later.

"Oh, and Grandma, maybe we could bake something when I come home from school."

"No argument from me! We can try a new recipe. Are you heading out, Martina?"

"I am. Duty calls."

Mom stared us both down. "You girls be safe."

We said our goodbyes, and I headed to the office to pick up Vincent and the rest of the team. I wanted to find Katie Kimble, and fast.

NESTLED in the bushes across the street from the warehouse, I used my binoculars to watch the comings and goings *for hours*. The other members of the team were snapping photos, on the lookout.

The soap factory.

With no movement all day, it seemed like the stakeout was a bust. But at dusk, lights in the building flickered on. What kind of soap factory only operated at night?

Not a soap factory.

With visibility low and a chill in the air, we switched out to our night-vision goggles. A few men and one woman had entered, but we didn't know who any of them were. No sign of Atlas. We'd have to run the photographs through facial recognition when we were back in the office.

Around 11 PM, Vincent radioed in. "It's our guy. He's here.

Just pulled into the parking lot in a blue SUV. He's in front of the building. He's not alone."

Through my binoculars, I spotted the SUV and said, "Confirmed."

Atlas walked with a man with dark hair, maybe six feet tall, well-built. He worked out; his large muscles were noticeable. As they were approaching the entrance, another man exited. The men's hands met in a brisk handshake. The new man was older, with brown and silver hair and a bit of a gut. Who were these people?

Soap manufacturers?

Not a chance.

The three men entered the building. Apparently, Atlas and this other man were who everyone was waiting for because an hour passed and nobody exited the building.

"I guess we stay until Atlas gets in his car and we can tail him. Or do we try to get in?" Vincent asked.

It was an open question because we hadn't decided. We were still waiting on blueprints for the building to see how we might get inside undetected. The smart thing to do was wait until we knew who the players were. We didn't want to go in completely blind.

Without warning, there was an incredibly loud whirring sound. It continued to get louder and louder. On the radio, I asked, "Do you hear that?"

"Oh, yeah, it's on the roof. There's a helicopter. It's taking off."

I glanced up, and sure enough, the helicopter blades were speeding up, and a few minutes later, the chopper lifted off the roof of the building, and whoever was inside was gone.

"Y'all just saw that, right?" Vincent asked.

"Yeah. That was definitely a helicopter taking off the roof of the *soap factory*."

What was Atlas into? This was bigger than the commune in Jenner. We had a man with a fake identity, someone who operated buildings in the middle of the night and then flew off in a chopper? What had we just stepped into?

20

———

FERN

"It's now or never," I said to myself, a sense of urgency taking hold. I had deliberated long and hard about my next steps. Yet, I couldn't help but wonder what life would be like on the outside. A life without Atlas, without our community. An unnerving realization dawned on me. Life on the outside could include a life on the run or in prison, and it was a frightening prospect. I had done horrible things. I couldn't deny that, and I wouldn't. It wouldn't be right. This time, I resolved to take responsibility for my actions, to lead an honorable life. It was what I'd always wanted.

As a child, I reveled in nature's simple pleasures. I loved playing with animals, hiking, picking flowers to decorate my hair or to put in a vase. When things were bad at home, I pretended to be somewhere else. In a field or a meadow. I swore when I left, I would no longer live with fear or violence. Yet, the decisions I'd made with Atlas meant I was likely to end up in prison, surrounded by hardened criminals. Did they feel remorse for their actions like I did?

Would life outside the community be worse than my

current situation? I didn't know what awaited me, but I was certain of one thing. I had to try. It was my only option.

From my vantage point by the window, I spotted Forrest engaged in a conversation with Cloud. I didn't know what they were discussing, but they looked distracted enough for me to make my move.

The plan was to climb out the bathroom window, discreetly exit the compound, and take my chances on the outside. Perhaps I could seek refuge on a nearby empty property or spend the night in the wilderness. Once they believed I was long gone, I could continue the journey during daylight. My options were limited, each fraught with danger. I could brave the dark, winding highway invisible to oncoming traffic or plunge into the ocean's watery depths. Either seemed preferable to living in fear, knowing any day he might see through me and decide to bury me right next to Opal.

Taking one last peek out the window, I decided it was go time. Quietly, I slid open the window and cautiously climbed out, holding my backpack in one hand. The one-story cabin was elevated, and the drop seemed daunting. I held my breath, jumped, and landed with a soft thud.

Frozen in place, I strained my ears for any sound that meant I'd been given away.

All was quiet. Too quiet, an ominous sign. Forrest and Cloud had ceased their conversation. I should've planned this better, perhaps crafted a diversion. As I remained still, the familiar creak of our cabin door made my heart pound. They were looking for me.

Taking a deep breath, I sprinted toward the property line. The sounds of yelling echoed behind me. They were calling for Atlas. I ignored it, focusing on my singular goal—escape.

The fence loomed ahead, six feet of solid obstacle, a daunting challenge for someone of my stature. My only option was the gate at the property's entrance. I sprinted along the fence line, the sound of footsteps growing louder behind me. As I neared the gate, my heart pounding in my chest, a figure came into view. It was Atlas.

Shaking his head, he asked, "Where are you going?"

Frozen, I stammered, "I just needed some air."

"With a backpack?" he countered, seeing right through me as he always did. "You need to come with me. We need to have a talk."

Was 'talk' a euphemism? Would it be like the 'talk' I'd had with Opal? Soon, Forrest and Huck loomed behind Atlas—his backup, his henchmen. There was no way I would get away. This was it; it was over. Atlas cocked his head and said, "Let's go back to the cabin, and we'll have a chat, okay?"

Glancing at my adversaries, I feigned calmness, my body shaking like the leaves in the towering trees above. "Okay, that's fine," I replied.

We walked back to the cabin in silence. Upon arriving, he instructed Huck and Forrest to leave us alone.

Inside, I perched on the edge of our bed and waited. He shut the door and approached me. "What were you doing out there?"

"I felt cooped up, trapped in here for days. You haven't visited. I needed to get out."

"And how do you think it would make me look if you just left all of us without saying a word?"

"I don't know." And quite frankly, I didn't care.

"I thought I could trust you with my heart, with my community, and now I feel that heart breaking. You've done that to me, Fern."

I swallowed. "That's not what I was trying to do."

"What were you trying to do? Hurt me? Why would you want to hurt me?"

"I don't want to hurt you. I don't want to hurt anybody, that's the point. After what happened, I can't live like this," I confessed.

"We went over that. She was going to destroy all of us. You did what you had to do. No, it wasn't pretty, and it's not something I'd wish upon anybody, but it was what we had to do. You did that for us. I thought you were one of us."

"But none of this is real!" I exclaimed, tears streaming down my face, terror gripping my insides. "You promised us peace and happiness in nature. Instead, you force sex on everybody, pretending like it's some sort of sharing of love. You kill people, you hurt people, and you control us. This is all fake!"

Atlas began pacing in front of me. "I'm really disappointed, Fern. And you know I can't have you ruining everything."

I gasped, realizing I was no match for Atlas or the others. This was it; it was over.

21

—————

MARTINA

Vincent and I huddled in the company car, studying blueprints of the warehouse. I pointed to one entrance and said, "Entering there should lead us to a stairwell. It may be our best option for getting in and out. From our surveillance, we've seen they use the front entrance, not the back."

"Agreed. It's the best option."

"Are you ready?"

Vincent pounded on his Kevlar vest. "As ready as I'm ever going to be." We were armed with lethal weapons, night vision goggles, and a small camera. Backup was parked a block over in case things got sticky, but at that point, we didn't know what we were stepping into, other than a warehouse rented by suspicious characters claiming to be making soap. I had to give Atlas credit. He was consistent with his cover of an earth-loving commune type by claiming to have a soap-making operation.

We slipped out of the vehicle and crouched down as we scurried along the fence line at the back of the property, behind the warehouse. There had been no activity for at least an hour, and no cars were in the parking lot—we suspected the place to be empty.

We jogged over to the back door. I pulled out my lock pick set and got to work. Within moments, we were inside. Vincent slowly closed the door behind us, trying not to make a sound in case we were wrong about the interior being empty.

Per the blueprints, there was a staircase directly in front of us. I lowered the goggles over my eyes, as did Vincent. I pointed downward. We were going to do a full perimeter search, starting with the bottom. Basements were notorious for dangerous activity, and this one didn't elicit positive thoughts.

Tiptoeing down the stairs, careful not to make any unnecessary noise, we reached the bottom of the stairwell and were met with a series of doors. Before they had rented the warehouse to Atlas, it was used as a storage facility for a linen distributor. Therefore, we didn't expect to find any illegal items left over from a previous tenant. If there was something suspicious inside, it was most certainly part of Atlas's operation.

I looked at Vincent and pointed to the door directly in front of us, signaling I would take the door to the right, and he could take the door to the left. In a hushed tone, I said, "Once we check the two rooms, we'll check the third together."

He nodded, and we set out on our separate missions.

Quietly entering the room with an unlocked door, I found the interior was pitch black. I pulled out a flashlight from my cargo pants and swept it across the four corners of the room. Empty. Unsure of what to expect, I hadn't expected an empty room. Certain there was nothing to be seen, I exited the room after turning off my flashlight.

I waited a moment for Vincent to emerge from his section. He was taking too long, and I worried about disturbing him by entering. After a minute, which seemed like an eternity, my fear got the better of me, and I entered the room.

Vincent was inside, flashlight illuminating pallets stacked with boxes. He turned his flashlight toward me, and I waved, letting him know I was a friendly. He waved his flashlight in the air as if summoning me to the edge of the room.

"What have you found?" I asked.

"Looks like boxes of soap."

"You're kidding," I said, incredulous.

"Nope. That's what the label says."

The label read Natural Herbal Soap Company.

Well, that was surprising.

"Perhaps they're hiding something in the soap boxes?" Vincent theorized.

"It's possible," I agreed. "Should we open one up?"

"Yeah, maybe one at the back."

We scurried around to the other side of the pallet near the far wall. I pulled out a knife from my pocket, flipped it open, and sliced open a box. The box contained individually wrapped bars of soap. I grabbed one of them, unwrapped the paper, and sniffed. "Lavender."

Using my knife to carve away at the soap to see if there was anything hidden within it, I sniffed again and shook my head. "It's just soap."

"They could easily mix it up, some real soap, some with stuff hidden inside," Vincent suggested.

It was a stretch. After I snapped a photo, I said, "If this is on the up and up, or even if it isn't, they'd have to be distributing it somewhere. We could search for the company name and major shipping routes to see if it's going somewhere."

"Smart," Vincent agreed. "I'll do that back in the office tomorrow."

I pointed to the other side of the room. "Did you inspect over there?"

"Yep. More soap. But if it's just soap, why would they keep it in the basement?"

"That's a good question." Were they preparing it for something? It was a lot of boxes to bring down there. "According to the blueprints, there should be an elevator on the other end of the hall. That must be how they got it down here."

Suddenly, my phone buzzed. Retrieving it from my pocket, I saw a message from Steve.

> Two cars pulled up. They're heading inside. At least three men.

Adrenaline pumping, I said, "We have to get out of here. We've got company."

I texted Steve back.

> Got it.

We set the soap down. What were three men doing at a soap factory at two in the morning? My guess was not making soap.

Thuds sounded from overhead.

We froze and switched off our flashlights. Footsteps echoed from the ceiling of the basement. Somebody had arrived, and they were right above us.

I whispered, "We need to get out of here quickly and quietly."

"I'll follow your lead."

Forging ahead, I stopped when we reached the door and listened.

The footsteps had quieted, which meant they were no longer near us. I turned the knob and stepped through, inching out of the room. I paused in between steps, listening.

With my hand, I signaled to Vincent to stop.

Footfall hurried toward us overhead, coming right toward the staircase.

In a flash, I hurried under the stairs with Vincent right

behind me. My heartbeat thudded in my ears as heavy boots pounded down the stairs, followed by another set. Mouthing a silent prayer, I waited.

22

MARTINA

A low voice echoed in the distance. "It's the door down here," one voice said to the other. "Okay, let's get the door propped open."

They proceeded toward the room we hadn't yet inspected. The man, I surmised, must have forced the door open and slid something underneath to keep it ajar. The sound of scraping was distinctive.

The man with the low voice said, "Okay, we'll carry the mattress down here, and then we'll bring her in."

Her? Were they holding someone captive here, or were they about to? I glanced at Vincent, and he tipped his chin, showing he'd caught their conversation as well.

In haste, the two men retraced their steps back up the stairs, returning a minute later carrying something that required both of them to maneuver down the staircase. Why hadn't they just taken the elevator? The footsteps made their way toward the far end of the hall. A thud echoed—a drop, maybe the mattress.

"Hey, there's an elevator right there!" one of them pointed out, to which the other responded, "He doesn't want any noise. It's our job to get her settled, then we get out of here."

"Okay."

They rushed back up the stairs, only to return shortly after. One of them headed back toward the room, the door still propped open. He placed something on the ground before hurrying back up the stairs.

Moments later, both men returned, visibly struggling with whatever they had been carrying down the stairs. Muffled cries filled the air—it was her, the woman they were talking about. They were bringing a woman into the room, intending to keep her captive.

A dreadful realization washed over me. Was this business a front for human trafficking? The cover of a soap factory provided the perfect disguise for hiding victims. It explained the extravagant expenses, like the helicopter—human trafficking was a lucrative business. Most soap factory executives didn't fly around in the dead of the night in a helicopter, but human traffickers certainly would.

They got the woman inside, even though she continued to struggle. A man muttered something under his breath, followed by a thump. I believed they must have dropped her onto the mattress on the floor.

"Pull her still!" one man ordered.

The sound of kicking ensued. She must've been struggling, trying to get out of their grasp. This went on for five seconds—I counted—and then silence fell.

"At last," one man said. "You heading home after this?"

"Not sure. I may have to meet them upstairs and discuss the plan. He told me he may have me stay behind and keep watch."

"Watch over what? She'll be out until tomorrow, for sure."

"Hey, I don't question him. I just do what he asks."

With that, they continued their brief conversation about the boss and their plans for the night. It was clear they had no intention of leaving the warehouse unattended. As much as I wanted to extract the woman who was obviously not in that room of her own accord, it was out of the question, at least for now. No case was worth dying for. I had a daughter to think about. We would have to come back for the woman.

I pulled out my phone and texted Steve.

> We're okay. They brought a woman in here and locked her in a room.

A message flashed on the screen.

> Get out. They're armed.

With the men back upstairs, we would have to leave the way we had come in. I showed the message to Vincent, and he nodded in agreement. About to crawl out from under the staircase, I froze when I heard footsteps approaching. I quickly pushed Vincent back into our hiding spot.

Another set of footsteps. "Did you hear something?"

"No, I didn't hear anything."

"Okay. He wants us to leave the stuff here and make sure she's out for the count before we leave."

I peeked out to get a look at the men. Though my view was limited, I noticed a bulge at the top of one man's jeans—a gun. Steve was right, we needed to get out of there.

Despite Vincent and I being armed and skilled, a firefight was the last thing we wanted.

"Okay, that should do it. She's out. She's got plenty of water. Let's go."

"You're not going to keep an eye on her?"

"No, he says he's got someone else for that."

"Cool." They hurried up the stairs, their footsteps becoming more and more faint.

I turned to Vincent. "Now."

Adrenaline pumping, I rushed up the stairs, out the back door, and didn't look back or stop until we were safely in my car. A text came in as I was catching my breath.

Nice work.

It was abundantly clear something dangerous was going on. There were men, guns, and a woman being held captive. It was enough to involve the police, who could take it from there. "How are you feeling?"

Vincent said, "Amped."

A dangerous situation had a way of doing that. "Let's get out of here."

"My thoughts exactly."

We pulled out of the neighborhood, figuring we had a few hours before they did whatever they were planning to do to that woman. They had obviously drugged her and had a plan for her. We needed to get back inside, preferably with the police, before it was too late.

23

HIRSCH

HUDDLED in a conference room with Jayda, Ross, a couple of narcotics officers, Sheriff Baldwin, and the research team, I waited for the update on the Sunny D deaths.

"Are we ready to get started?" Jayda asked.

"I think everyone's here."

Jayda's head dipped in a single decisive move, telling Ross to project the slides. My knowledge of the situation was limited, but I was aware the team had a few developments and a proposal on how to proceed. I suspected it might be a suggestion to hire outside consultants because of the high-profile nature of the case. I'd broached the subject with Sheriff Baldwin, but I hadn't convinced him it was necessary yet. Regardless, I was eager to solve the case before another life was lost.

The press conference had been helpful, or so we thought. There had been no deaths since, and we hoped the dealers were nervous, pushing them underground. Perhaps they would even grow a conscience and update their lethal formula to stop killing their customers. The last update I received showed we had made no headway; we didn't have any leads. Zander was being held for his own protection, and I was still negotiating with the district attorney about his charges. Sending a young man like Zander into a general population prison would not only cost him his life but also ruin any chance he had to turn his life around. Prison, with its most dangerous criminals, would only transform Zander into one of them.

"Great. Thanks for coming," Jayda began. "As you know, Ross and I have taken the lead on the Sunny D deaths. The team has been working non-stop to find the dealers responsible. Based on advice from Dr. Katarina Dobbs in our forensics department, we believe it's crucial to find the source of the drugs. Since it's considered designer and it's the first we've seen of it, we think it's essential. With that, I'm going to hand this over to Rosemary from the research team to tell us what she and the team have found."

Rosemary stood up and said, "Thanks, Jayda. Based on the street interviews, we've been able to collect multiple samples of Sunny D. We made a plea with a few known buyers for samples. The news coverage helped with the cooperation. We got samples from six months, three months, one month, three weeks, and a week ago. What Kiki's team... oh, sorry." She blushed. "Dr. Katarina Dobbs' team found the formulations are not the same. The LSD, or lysergic acid diethylamide formula, concentration, and purity, are identical. The fentanyl formula and purity are also nearly equivalent. However, the concentration is a different story. Until a month ago, the concentration of fentanyl was the same. It wasn't until the samples from three weeks ago and one week ago that the fentanyl concentration was fifty percent higher than the previous lots."

I felt like I was understanding, but to be sure, I said, "What you're saying is the drugs weren't lethal until three weeks ago."

Rosemary bobbed her head up and down, her green eyes sparkling. "Exactly."

"Which corresponds with when the first death was reported," I noted.

Sheriff Baldwin interjected, "The drug has only been killing people for a few weeks?"

"That's right," Jayda confirmed. "It fits the pattern. But based on what Rosemary and Kiki's team found, the consensus is that it's the same manufacturer. However, the new formula is off."

"Any way to trace the materials?" the sheriff asked.

"Based on the chemical makeup and purity, it has to be the same manufacturer," Rosemary reiterated.

"If we find who is making it, we can bring down the organization?" Sheriff Baldwin questioned.

"Yeah, but we have a feeling it's a pretty large organization," Jayda replied.

This was news to me. "Why do we think that?"

"Well, we finally got another break that might lead us to just that," Jayda explained, as Ross advanced the slide to a dark photo of a few cars in a parking lot.

"Thanks, Rosemary," Jayda said, to which Rosemary smiled sheepishly and took her seat.

As our top researcher, Rosemary was a valuable asset, especially considering she was a friend of Kiki, the head of the forensics lab, and collaborated with her often. It was good news for us, as Rosemary could present both the forensics and research findings.

Jayda continued, "The streets have been pretty quiet since the press release. We haven't spotted anybody dealing Sunny D. But we have been keeping round-the-clock surveillance on Ashworth, or 'Ash,' who was re-upping our street dealers. We lucked out when he finally went somewhere other than McDonald's and the corner liquor store."

Jayda pointed to the screen. "We followed him here. As you can see, he was meeting up with some 'friends.'"

Ross added, "Middle-of-the-night meeting friends."

"Drug dealers," Sheriff added.

"Most likely," Jayda confirmed.

"Any identifications?" I asked.

"These are hot off the press. Rosemary's team is running them through facial recognition, but we're not sure the resolution of the photos is good enough to get a hit," Jayda explained.

Sheriff Baldwin asked, "Have you presented any of this to the DEA?"

"Not yet. We think that might be our next step. Just because we don't know these guys, it doesn't mean they're not known to the DEA. We don't know anything about them. Maybe they're bringing in the drugs from Mexico or somewhere overseas," Jayda suggested.

Sheriff Baldwin said, "I've got contacts at the DEA. I can set up a meeting. Some solid folks who will share information."

As much as Sheriff Baldwin and I got along over the years, I didn't want to steal his thunder and tell him we had our share of contacts with the DEA. During our time at the cold case squad, we had run-ins with a few of them. A few of those DEA agents had saved our lives and helped solve our cases.

"What's the current theory?" I asked, eager for a breakthrough.

Jayda pointed at the screen of a man standing across from Ashworth. "We think this guy here is the next level up from Ash."

"Do you have a name?" I questioned further.

"We do, but he doesn't have a criminal record."

Ross stood up and pointed to a man with dark hair and a noticeable gut. "This guy here isn't in our database, but he's got quite a few associates. These are a couple of faces we'd like to show to the DEA. Not to profile, but they don't look like our typical cartel types except for the guy tatted up."

There were a lot of head nods in the conference room. The team was going in the right direction. I could feel it—we were close to learning more. Sheriff said, "Any idea what's inside?"

"No, we don't have any eyes on the inside, but we could take pictures of Ash and the shady-looking associates," Ross explained.

Rosemary piped in, "We're also doing a full background on the property and license plates. We should have information by the end of the day. It's a lot to process."

"Nice work." That's what happens when you have a great team.

Ross gave a lopsided grin. "But, to be honest, we think we know how to break this case wide open."

Picking up a vibe, I watched Ross, who eyed Jayda. They both had a look I couldn't quite decipher. A tell. The punchline was coming. "Jayda, would you like to do the honors?"

The scene reminded me of the days with the Cold Case Squad. All working together with a common goal. Camaraderie.

"With pleasure," she responded enthusiastically.

The slide changed to a photo of two figures outside the building, away from Ash and his associates. "The team took these in the early hours of the morning. We think these two may be the key to breaking this case wide open." Jayda flipped the slide again, and a blown-up picture of the two figures appeared.

Nearly speechless, I said, "I'll make a call."

24

———

MARTINA

Yawning, I said, "Morning, Vincent."

"Is it still morning?"

"Clock says ten," I confessed. "Feels like it should be midnight. I have to admit, I'm ready for a nap."

After the early hour adrenaline rush, I barely got any sleep. But it felt good to be out in the field, heart pumping, trying to catch the bad guys and find our missing person. My thoughts went back to that woman locked in the room. Who was she? Was her family looking for her? What were Atlas and his crew going to do with her? I didn't have any contacts in the Sonoma County Sheriff's Department, so I decided to call Hirsch to see if he knew anyone to let them know what we found, and hopefully, they could go in and rescue the woman.

Part of me wasn't sure what to do, though. We still hadn't found Katie. Would helping this woman take away our chances of finding Katie? I wasn't sure, but I couldn't *not* help the woman. With a silent prayer, I vowed to try to save them both.

Considering I had broken in and entered the building, I'd have to be careful who I reported it to. I supposed I could report it anonymously, but I'd rather have a conversation with Hirsch about it.

"Did you get any sleep last night?" I asked.

"A little, but honestly, the adrenaline kept me pumped, making sleep a bit challenging, you know?"

"I know."

"How about you?"

"A couple hours."

I'd only been in the office a few minutes when Stavros approached my door.

"How did it go last night?" he asked.

"It was interesting." I filled in Stavros, my business partner, former boss, and family friend, on what we discovered at the warehouse in the early hours.

"Any idea how this may relate to your missing person, Katie Kimble?"

"We know the boyfriend is into something illegal, between the helicopters and the clandestine meetings in the middle of the night. Something's not right there. Maybe human trafficking. If that's the case, he could have trafficked Katie. It's just a theory, though."

"Dangerous. You've got plenty of backup if you need it."

"Noted. In a minute, I'll call Hirsch and see how to handle the legality of it all. There's a woman who needs our help. It can't be legal what they're doing to her."

"Tread carefully. Talk in generalities with Hirsch. What you did wasn't exactly legal; he may be obligated."

"Understood." That was one drawback of being a PI as opposed to working with the police department. I knew there was a woman in danger, but I had no evidence, and I only knew about it because I had committed a crime by breaking into the building.

Then again, the police could break and enter without losing

their jobs—if they had a warrant or probable cause. Definitely pros and cons of working at the sheriff's department and working for my firm. Although, I didn't miss all the rules and regulations of the sheriff's department. At Drakos Monroe, we made our decisions based on what was best for our clients.

The phone on my desk rang. I picked it up. "Hello."

"Martina, how are you doing this morning?" came the response.

Puzzled by his chipper demeanor, I said, "It was a long night. What's up?" I lowered the phone and mouthed 'It's Hirsch,' to Vincent and Stavros. Stavros lifted his hand, waved, and exited. I gestured for Vincent to sit down.

"I bet. You know, if you're not too busy, I was hoping to meet with you."

"Meet with me?"

"Yeah, you got me thinking about your missing person's case."

"Yeah?" I was intrigued.

"I think we can help."

His statement took me by surprise. "What a coincidence. I was hoping to talk to you about that case." Neither Hirsch nor I believed in coincidences.

"Anyway, could you come down to the sheriff's department and have a meeting with me and a few others?" Hirsch asked.

He was being cagey. What did he have up his sleeve? "What's going on, Hirsch?"

"Do you trust me, Martina?"

"Do I trust you?" I repeated, staring into Vincent's curious eyes. "With my life."

"Can you be down here in an hour?"

My pulse sped up. "I can."

"Can you bring Vincent with you?"

Eying Vincent, I said, "Yeah, Vincent's available."

Vincent cocked his head.

"I'll see you in an hour." Hirsch hung up.

Vincent asked, "What was that about?"

"He wants us down at the sheriff's department in an hour to meet with him and a few others. Thinks he can help us with our case."

"Really? And he didn't say how?"

"No."

He looked up and then said, "Do you trust him?"

"He has a history of keeping things close to the chest," I admitted.

"Want to grab a cup of coffee before we head out?" Vincent proposed.

"Absolutely."

VINCENT and I strutted through the doors of the oh-so-familiar CoCo County Sheriff's Department and waved at a young man behind the reception desk I didn't recognize. It was odd not knowing the person behind the desk. I wondered what had happened to Gladys. Maybe she worked a different shift? She was no spring chicken; I hoped her absence didn't mean she was no longer with us, both at the sheriff's department and in this world.

At the reception desk, I said, "Hi, my name is Martina Monroe, and this is Vincent Teller. We're here to see Sergeant Hirsch."

The young man smiled brightly. "Wow, the famous Martina and Vincent. So good to meet you. My name is Carl. I'm new."

"Nice to meet you, Carl."

"Sergeant Hirsch said to have you go to conference room one as soon as you got here."

What on earth was Hirsch having us walk into?

"I presume you know the way," Carl said.

"That we do." It used to be the cold case squad room. What was Hirsch up to?

Vincent and I approached the door, and I knocked, which felt weird. In all my years at the sheriff's department, I never had to knock; it had been like I owned the place. Being a visitor was uncomfortable, and I didn't love it.

The door opened, and Hirsch greeted us. "Martina, Vincent, so glad you're here. Come on in." After a quick pat on the shoulder, Hirsch ushered us in. "Please, have a seat."

Scanning the room, I noticed several bright faces, some familiar, some new to us. Most surprisingly, Sheriff Baldwin, Jayda, and Ross were present.

Apprehensively, we sat down. I felt like I was being pranked or something similar; it was like everyone knew what was going on but Vincent and me.

Hirsch said, "Can I get you a coffee or water before we get started?"

"We're as caffeinated as we probably should be. Any more and we may start buzzing. Go ahead and get to it," I responded.

Hirsch remained standing and leaned against the wall. "Most people in this room are very familiar with the one and only Martina Monroe and, of course, Vincent Teller. Martina, the two folks at the end are Kiva and Rourke; they're part of our narcotics team. Of course, you remember Rosemary, Jayda, Ross, and Sheriff Baldwin."

"Of course. I have a feeling this is going to be interesting, Hirsch."

He chuckled, as did half the room.

"As most of you know, Ms. Monroe and Mr. Teller used to work with the cold case squad here in CoCo County. Now, they're both private investigators. Martina is co-owner of Drakos

Monroe Security & Investigations, and if you don't know, they're one of the most well-respected security and investigation firms in the state of California, if not the entire United States. You want security, you want investigations done, you call Drakos Monroe."

The room made rumblings, showing they'd heard of us. Eagerly awaiting Hirsch's big announcement, I stared at him.

"Well, Martina and I are friends. I think everybody knows that. And sometimes we like to talk shop. Martina was telling me she and Vincent have been working on a missing persons case. I told her, and the rest of the Bay Area, that we're working on five deaths associated with LSD laced with fentanyl. Street name: Sunny D."

I knew Hirsch, and if I was correct, he'd found something.

He pointed at the projector, and it came alive with images of the warehouse in Santa Rosa. I looked at him and then at the screen. He stood smiling with the silliest grin I'd ever seen on his face. I said, "Okay, we're listening."

Hirsch explained the surveillance they'd done on Ashworth, a dealer of Sunny D. They'd tracked the dealers who supplied Ashworth with the drug, who they thought was a man with long hair and a bushy beard.

"So, these photographs are from surveillance early this morning. And boy, were we surprised when we saw two familiar characters rushing out of the warehouse around 2 AM."

Vincent and I exchanged glances. I doubted this entire ruse was to throw us in jail, but boy, did I have a feeling we were about to be caught red-handed.

Jayda flipped the image on the screen. "Imagine our surprise when we saw these two." It was a magnified photo of Vincent and me running outside the building. The team snickered.

Blushing, I said, "Are we under arrest?"

Sheriff Baldwin laughed. "Absolutely not. We can pretend we don't know that you didn't have permission to go inside."

"True, you don't know that. Maybe I'm good friends with the owner of the warehouse."

"That's right. A delightful fellow directed us to the warehouse. Goes by the name Jeff," Vincent added.

Hirsch stepped forward and said, "What we're thinking, which is pretty obvious at this point, is you're exploring the warehouse as part of your missing person investigation."

"That's right. We're following Katie Kimble's boyfriend, the guy with the long hair and beard, and this is where he led us. We have surveillance from a few different days of him coming and going from the warehouse. Last night, we went inside to learn more about what's going on."

Vincent said, "We know his fake identity is Jackson Galen, but we're completely in the dark as to who he really is. The guy's a ghost."

"Yep. This guy lives in Jenner, up the coast, has a commune with a bunch of hippies. They grow their own vegetables, that kind of thing."

"Why did you follow him?" Ross asked.

"Because we sensed something was off about the commune. Within moments of pulling up, a commune member greeted us. Like a lookout. The first two times we visited, Atlas—Katie's boyfriend—wasn't there. But the third time, he was, and he gave us a tour. Told us to come and stay. He was convincing, even gave us a glass of iced tea with lemons from their trees."

"It was the best iced tea I'd ever had," Vincent said, and the room laughed.

"It was good iced tea, but something seemed off, disingenuous. So, we started following Atlas—he goes by the name Atlas. We didn't buy his story that he didn't know where Katie was.

He said he hadn't talked to her in two years, which is how long she's been missing."

Sheriff Baldwin added, "You assumed if you found out more about the boyfriend, you'd find out what happened to Katie?"

"Exactly."

"And what have you found so far?"

"Well, you're saying he's associated with Sunny D, the designer drug that's killing people? I guess it's drugs. We were inside the warehouse last night; we only made it downstairs to the basement. In one room, they're storing pallets of soap—natural, lavender-scented soap."

"Soap?"

"Yes, and now that we're hearing there's drugs, it's likely they're transporting the drugs in the soap. But not only did we find the soap, which didn't hold any drugs, but we also heard them bring a woman into a room. We think she's drugged and locked in the room. I was going to call you Hirsch because I wanted to figure out how to handle it. She's in danger."

"I'm glad you came to us because it could jeopardize the entire investigation if another organization goes in guns blazing."

Letting this all sink in, I realized Katie's boyfriend was a drug dealer, and everything else was a front. Who was he really, and where did he come from?

"What do you know about the people Atlas is meeting with?" I asked.

"Nothing yet. We're following this guy." Ross reverted the slides to a man meeting with Atlas. "This guy does re-ups to the dealers on the street, so we've been following him. We think Atlas is the next guy up in the chain."

I said, "The chain may go pretty high. A couple of nights ago, we were there, and they left off the roof in a helicopter."

"Based on some images of the associates and their tattoos, we're thinking maybe drug cartels. This is big."

I said, "Have you brought any of this to the DEA yet?"

Sheriff Baldwin smirked. "I asked the same question."

Were we just sharing information, or was there more going on in this room? "It sounds like our cases are connected. The boyfriend of my missing person is part of the drug organization you're hunting down." I turned to Hirsch.

He said, "The sheriff, the team, and I have been talking. We would like to make a formal request for your services to help us in the Sunny D deaths. They're connected to your case anyway, and we could use you and Vincent full time on this. The minds we have in this room are what we need to solve this case, get these drugs off the street, and save innocent lives."

A little stunned, I waited.

The sheriff said, "I know you both can do the job. And please know, this wasn't a light decision. We need you. We know what you're capable of, and you know I have the highest respect for both of you and appreciate so much what you've already done for CoCo County. I still wish I had the budget for you—not that I think you would take us back full time—but we're hoping you'll help us with this case. Maybe it's the beginning of a new type of relationship with CoCo County and Drakos Monroe Security & Investigations. Perhaps you'd be willing to come on under special circumstances when we need a particular task force, when we need the best of the best to solve the toughest cases. I'm not promising anything, but the way I see this is as a trial run."

He wanted to contract us for a case they couldn't handle on their own. I looked at Vincent; I could tell by the look in his eyes he wanted it, and he wanted it bad. With a knowing glance toward Vincent, I turned to Hirsch and said, "Let's do it."

25

FERN

MY EYELIDS FLUTTERED as I touched my fingertips to the top of my head. I turned, trying to decipher my surroundings, but found nothing but pitch black. With a sense of foreboding, I wondered where I was and how long I'd been there. My head swimming, I attempted to sit up, only to quickly lie back down. *They must've drugged me.* This sensation was not a pleasant trip. Was this hell? Was I dead? I pinched my arm and inhaled the musty scent of the mattress beneath me. Not dead.

My escape had been flawed. In this new reality, I knew I'd rather be a prisoner in my home, in the cabin I shared with Atlas, where I had the comforts of clean sheets, sunlight, and running water, than this dark, dank place. My throat tightened as I swallowed hard. I desperately needed a drink of water.

I ran my fingers along the mattress and onto the cold concrete floor, and hope filled me as my fingertips brushed against a plastic bottle. After a squeeze, I was convinced it contained water. Even prisoners got water, right? I pushed myself to my hands and knees, opened the bottle, and discarded the cap onto the floor. Not entirely convinced it was clean water, I took a cautious sip, fearing it could be something awful —poison, or worse. I wasn't sure what could be worse.

Relief flooded me. It tasted like water, and I took another sip, then a gulp. Before I knew it, more than half the bottle was gone. I set it down, uncertain when I would get more. What were they going to do with me? Why had I made so many mistakes? I should've pretended that everything was okay, been more patient, and not tried to fight Atlas, Huck, Forrest, or any of them.

In the future, I needed to be smarter and think about the situation rationally. I lay back down, resting my woozy head. I knew I should've planned better, but in my desperation, I thought running would be enough. But it wasn't. I had to get back on Atlas's good side. Make him believe I was upset but that I'd changed my mind. But not too quickly, so it was believable. And when the time was right, I would attempt to escape. My escape plan would have to be put on hold, but the wait would be worth it. I only hoped I'd get the chance.

Footsteps approached.

Fear propelled me until I was cowering against the wall, making myself even smaller. The door opened, and a flood of light invaded my senses. I covered my eyes, momentarily blinded. "How did you sleep?" a familiar voice asked. It was Atlas.

Relieved, I mumbled, "Like a baby." My voice was hoarse from dehydration and fear.

"We have to go. Get on your feet."

Knowing better than to argue, I slowly stood, using the wall to prop myself up. "Where are we going?"

"Don't ask questions. We're going now." He took my hand, a surprisingly gentle gesture. It was strange, these mixed emotions I had toward Atlas. I feared and loved him at the same time. How could I still love him? I wrapped my arms around him and squeezed, longing for his body's warmth. He pushed me back slightly. "We have to get out of here."

"Okay." I kept my arm around him so he could help me up the stairs and down the hallway. We were at the warehouse. I had been there on enough occasions to know there wasn't anything terribly sinister to be worried about unless other people were there. It didn't appear there was.

Atlas helped me along, and we made it outside to the parking lot. He opened the passenger door and assisted me inside. He fastened my seat belt—an unexpected act of concern if he was planning to kill me.

Once in the car, he shut the door and sped off without a word. As we made our way down the highway, I finally asked, "What's going on, Atlas?"

"Have you had time to think?" he asked, his voice emotionless.

Oh, had I ever. "Yes, I have."

"And do you still want to leave me?" He glanced at me.

"No, I'm so sorry. I was going a little nuts in that cabin by myself, but I realize now it was foolish. I'm so sorry. What have you told the others?"

"Glad to hear you've come to your senses. I've told the community we're on a trip. It should be fine." His response was monotone, devoid of any emotion.

Was he going to forgive me just like that? "I'm so sorry, Atlas. Do you forgive me?" A pang of hope echoed in my voice.

He peeked over at me and then returned his gaze to the road. "I'll need you to prove it."

My heart sank. What did he mean by that? "Anything. I'll do anything. Please, don't leave me, Atlas."

"We have to go somewhere. There are some people who are not happy with things." He turned and looked at me, his eyes filled with a fear I hadn't seen before. "Dangerous people are nervous, and that's not good for us."

Atlas was scared. The only one I could think who could elicit that emotion was the head. We didn't talk about him much, but I'd met him, and he was an intimidating figure for sure. He had been friendly because we were making him a lot of money, but I could only imagine being on his bad side.

"Where are we going?" I asked, my voice barely above a whisper.

"To a motel. We'll stay there a few days until I figure some things out."

"Okay." I didn't know what he meant by "figure some things out" but for now, it seemed like I was protected from danger. But if the head was upset with Atlas, neither one of us was safe.

26

———

MARTINA

SITTING IN THE CONFERENCE ROOM, now referred to as the Sunny D task force room, I glanced across the space at Hirsch, who paced while talking on his cell phone. Our eyes met, and he smiled ever so slightly. He was as happy as I was to be back in the game, working together at the sheriff's department. It wouldn't last forever, but nothing truly great did. We could enjoy it and save lives at the same time. We'd spent the better part of the day strategizing on how to capture those responsible for the recent deaths and find Katie Kimble.

Unsure of who Hirsch was talking to, I hoped he was on the phone with the Sonoma County Sheriff's Department with an update on the warehouse in Santa Rosa where we'd seen the suspected drug dealers and the woman being held captive. They said they would patrol the area while not arousing suspicion.

Despite my weary bones, the case exhilarated me. Other than being a little shaky from too much caffeine, it felt good to be in the middle of it, working with an exceptional team.

Drakos Monroe was great. It just wasn't the same. There was something special about having both law enforcement and private investigators working together. Different perspectives, law-abiding citizens and those who'd bent a few rules now and again. It was no surprise to anyone Vincent had joined the PI side. He and I had worked the gray areas a few times while working at the sheriff's department. It was, of course, for the good of the victims, but we'd still found ourselves in some hot water.

Hirsch hung up the phone and hurried over. "That was the Sonoma County Sheriff's Department. They went to the warehouse. It's locked up and there's nobody there."

"Did they go inside?"

"They can't, without a warrant."

"But can't they enter if they believe someone inside is in danger?"

"Only if they can argue imminent danger in front of a judge. But how do you prove there's someone who might be in danger without saying a friend broke in and heard some things?"

It was another reminder of why I wasn't in law enforcement. Nodding, I said, "So, it's up to the non-law enforcement folks to solve this one."

He let out a sigh. "There were no cars at the warehouse, which likely means they've moved whoever was in that room. You said someone was guarding her, right?"

"Yes." He had a point. It wasn't likely she was still in that room, unless they'd killed her and felt there was no reason to guard the building anymore. But considering I knew how to get in pretty quickly, perhaps I should take a look for myself.

"What is the Sonoma County Sheriff going to do next? Are they going to surveil the warehouse, wait for someone to show up, and then ask if they can look around?"

"Officially, they have no reason to look. But they said they'll keep patrol. They'll swing in every so often and call us if they see anything." The strategy reeked of classic law enforcement protocol—a wait-and-see approach. It was one of my least favorite approaches, especially when I knew someone was in danger.

"There could be a woman in imminent danger, but because we don't have a warrant, we're going to let her die?" I snapped.

Hirsch gave me a look. I knew it was harsh, but he had to understand a woman's life was at stake. He glanced up at the wall, studying the clock. "It's an hour and a half from here. Maybe you should take an early dinner break," he suggested. "I can hold down the fort here, contact the DEA."

That's my partner. "I'm hungry. Hey, Vincent, you hungry?"

He looked puzzled. "I could eat."

And that's why we worked together so well. Hirsch and I could communicate with no words at all. "Great idea, Hirsch. I'm gonna take a break." I stood up and patted him on the arm. "Us little PIs'll see you in a bit."

He gave a half-grin, clearly amused. "See you soon."

Hirsch didn't have to tell me I was free to break into the warehouse to check it out. I knew him and he knew me. It was the magic of our partnership. Being a PI, I could do things outside the law, and considering no paperwork had been signed, I wasn't technically under contract with the sheriff's department. And therefore, I wasn't acting on their behalf. Vincent and I were 100% Drakos Monroe Security & Investigations.

Vincent and I hurried out of the sheriff's department, and once in the car, he said, "We're hungry?"

"Hirsch talked to the Sonoma County Sheriff's Department. They don't think they have enough probable cause to go in and see if that woman is okay."

"So, we're going to go bring her some dinner?"

I gave him a look, like *don't be dense.* "We're going to go check on her ourselves."

"But we risk going into a firefight, right?"

"The Sonoma County Sheriff's Department said there are

no cars outside the warehouse, so either she's not there anymore, or she doesn't have a guard on her. If there is a car, we'll leave and call the sheriff's department. They said if there's a car or other sign someone is there, they'll go over and ask to look around."

"Sneaky. I like it."

Both of us were alive and functioning solely on adrenaline and caffeine. He had dark circles under his eyes, and I was sure I looked atrocious, but it didn't matter. There was a woman who needed us, and we wouldn't stop until we helped her.

On the drive, I asked Vincent what he thought of this gig. "It's pretty cool working with the team again. I admit, I miss it."

"I think we all do."

"You think they'll be able to re-form a team?"

"Not likely, but one-offs, and maybe a special task force. I could see that in the future. But I'm a partner at the company. I can't be full time at the sheriff's department. However, you probably have an opportunity if it arises. If that's what you want. But the sheriff is pretty adamant he doesn't have the budget for a full-time consultant, so I wouldn't keep your hopes up."

"It'd be cool to work with them from time to time, like on a really big, tough case. Those are the best ones, anyway."

True. "You've been thinking about your future a lot, huh?" We hadn't had a chance to circle back to the conversation we'd had about Amanda and his future.

"Yeah, why do you ask?"

Subtlety was not my strong suit. "Just curious is all. I think you and Amanda are great together."

"Yeah, we are. I just... I know she's my person, Martina. But I'm not sure I'm ready for all of it. Wife. Kids. Picket fence. I mean, if it was just saying, 'Amanda, you and me forever, let's take the world by storm,' I wouldn't hesitate. But the baby thing... babies are so much, aren't they?"

I chuckled. "You're not wrong, Vincent. Children take up a lot of time, energy, love, patience and, yeah, things change when you have kids, but you get to decide how much changes. Will you be globetrotting with a newborn? Probably not. Can you still have this job with a child? Absolutely."

"I can see that. But, I mean, look at Hirsch. He took a desk job and is a sergeant now. I don't want that."

Hirsch, yeah, he was a different one. "True, he did that, but you see how energized he is working on this case. He's alive. And maybe he only works a case under special circumstances. He made a choice. He wanted to be there for Audrey's firsts. Now she's a little older, and the nanny helps him to still have time with Kim and the job. Your life isn't over when you have children. It just changes, and it can change in a really good way."

"Okay, I believe you, I guess."

I glanced at him quickly. "Talk to Amanda. Tell her what your fears are. Maybe she doesn't want a baby right now. Maybe she wants one in two years, maybe three years, or maybe she doesn't know exactly when."

"You're right. I clam up when she brings up the topic. I should talk to her."

"You really should, especially if, like you said, she is your person. You should share all your feelings with her. Let her understand and then ask her how she feels. You never know. As much as I love Zoey and was so happy when she was born, I was terrified when I found out I was pregnant. She was about ten years earlier than Jared and I had planned. You never know, Amanda may want a baby but could also be scared to be a mom. If you share your feelings with her, she's more likely to share her feelings with you."

Vincent said, "You're very wise, Martina."

I laughed.

"I'm serious."

"Sure you are. But I won't lie. Sometimes I do things the hard way."

"I see that. But thanks. It's nice to have someone to talk to about it."

"Any time. This case has us spending a lot of time together, so if you need more wisdom or there's anything you want to talk about, I'm always here."

Vincent grew serious and said, "I appreciate that, Martina."

As we approached the area of the warehouse, I said, "There's no cars."

"Nope, none from last night."

"Okay, I'll park in the same spot. We'll run fast, peek in, check the room, and get out, undetected."

"Aye aye, boss," he said with a smile.

Parked, I suited up and rushed over to the warehouse, familiar with the doors and locks. We hurried down the stairs, our footsteps echoing through the hallway. If there was anybody there, they'd hear us, but that wasn't our concern today. It was about getting the woman out to safety.

We reached the door. It was open and the room was empty. A sinking feeling washed over me. "She's gone."

"I don't see any signs of struggle. Maybe they transferred her."

With a sense of defeat, I said, "It's possible."

We'd lost her, whoever she was.

"Let's get out of here." Frustrated with myself and the sheriff's department, I felt sick for handing the woman over to her captors and not going back for her sooner. *I know one thing for sure; I won't let it happen again.*

27

———————

MARTINA

WITH ALMOST A FULL night's sleep, I was ready to do it all over again. It had been a stretch since I'd pulled an all-nighter, worked all day, and then crashed. The lingering fatigue made me think I was getting too old for this. When I walked into the task force room, I noticed Vincent had beaten me to the office. Hirsch was already there, bright-eyed, ready to take on the Sunny D drug organization. "Good morning, task force," I said with enthusiasm.

"Good morning. I'm guessing you've already had your coffee?"

I lifted the travel mug my mom had prepared for me. Knowing I'd be working nonstop, she'd stayed overnight the last few nights to help take care of the house, Barney, and Zoey. Even though Zoey argued because she was sixteen, she didn't need anybody to take care of her. She'd been telling me that since she was seven years old. Granted, she was older and could take care of herself a lot more than she used to. But she was still only sixteen and needed a parental figure around. "What's new?"

"The DEA says they're swamped. The earliest they can

meet with us is Monday, and that's if their current operation goes well."

"Monday? I don't think that woman has until Monday or..."

I didn't like that we couldn't meet with the DEA sooner, but obviously they had full-time jobs, too. We were asking for a favor, to identify our suspects because we couldn't. "Maybe they took her to the Jenner commune."

Hirsch said, "It's possible."

"I've been thinking a lot about this," I began, my voice echoing slightly in the quiet of the room. "I'm guessing the commune is riddled with secrets. What if I go undercover? Atlas invited us to come stay anytime we wanted. I could go in, wear some linen clothes, maybe a cotton T-shirt, till some soil, and get a good look around."

Hirsch shot me a look, his eyes widening. "Martina, you're talking about going undercover by yourself to a 20-acre property owned by a known drug dealer, who we think is capable of violence."

When he put it like that, it sounded dangerous. I let out an exasperated breath. It was risky, and if they were as threatening as we thought, going in unarmed and unprotected was a bad idea. "What other choice do we have?" I asked, more to myself than to anyone else.

"Aerial surveillance," Vincent suggested.

Aerial surveillance was an option. We couldn't see around the property, but we could probably see from above it. "Is that something we have access to?" I asked Hirsch.

"It's not standard, but this is a pretty big deal. The problem is, once we run helicopters and aerial surveillance, they're going to see it and they're going to hear it. It could blow the whole thing."

What were we to do? Sit around and wait until this woman,

who had been held captive, just showed up? "So, what do we do?" I asked, frustration evident in my voice.

Jayda and Ross strolled in. "Good morning, team. It's so good to see you," Jayda said.

"Good to see you too," I responded. "We've hit a snag. The DEA can't meet with us until Monday, and we're trying to figure out a way inside the commune in Jenner. Vincent suggested aerial surveillance, but that'll be tricky. They'll hear a helicopter."

Ross sat down with a thud and set his greasy bag on top of the table. I had succeeded in getting Hirsch off fast food, but Ross was hopeless. He pulled out a sandwich and unwrapped it, his gaze fixed on the paper. "What about drones?"

"Drones?" I was surprised by the suggestion.

"Why didn't I think of that?" Vincent asked.

"Because you're younger and less experienced than me," Ross replied, half teasing.

"No, I just need more caffeine." Vincent chortled.

"Okay, okay, whoever's idea it is, let's talk more about these drones. How do we set that up?" Hirsch asked.

Yes. I loved the idea of drones. We'd be able to check out the compound without putting the team in harm's way. Gotta love working with a smart team.

"The firm has drones, right, Martina?" Vincent asked.

"Yes, we have some pretty cool stuff in our equipment warehouse. Drones are perfect. We have smaller ones; they may not see them. The small drones will look like birds flying around. And better yet, they'll have no clue whose they are, so even if they recognize them, maybe they won't suspect it's the police or us looking for Katie. I think it can work. I like it."

"And no one gets hurt," Hirsch added.

Hirsch, ever the protector. It would be dangerous to go undercover by myself, unarmed, into a drug organization.

Although, I had a feeling the members of the commune weren't all drug dealers. They seemed so peaceful; like they wouldn't hurt a fly. But I had heard the woman, her struggle, and her muffled cries. Atlas and his associates were shady, but how shady was unclear.

Vincent spoke up. "I'll call the equipment team. We'll figure out a strategy to deploy the drones and check out the footage."

This was why having many minds in one room was so effective. I hadn't done aerial surveillance in forever, not since my Army days, and I hadn't thought of it. Great minds, great solutions.

"All right, let's head back over to Drakos Monroe. We'll talk to the equipment team, and we'll keep in touch."

Hirsch said, "Great. We'll talk soon."

With that, we had a plan. Hopefully, one where none of the team would get hurt. I couldn't wait to see what those drones found. Would they find our missing person? Uncover more details about the drug operation?

28

MARTINA

The sunshine poured down as I refilled my glass with iced tea. It was a beautiful spring day, and my favorite people in the entire world surrounded me. Holding my full glass, I turned to watch as Zoey, Audrey, and Barney chased each other around on the grass. Audrey's giggles reverberated throughout the back yard. She was adorable, a perfect combination of Hirsch and Kim—a blonde-haired, blue-eyed girl with angelic features and an adorable personality.

Kim approached. "It's quite the sight, isn't it?"

"It is. You may need to get Audrey a puppy," I teased.

"I don't know if we could handle a puppy, too."

"Fair enough. I got cornered by my mom and Zoey for a week before they convinced me we should adopt Barney. But he's great company, and I'm glad we did. Sometimes we have things that come into our life, and we don't know what kind of impact they're going to have."

I hadn't been completely keen on adding a puppy to our lives, but Barney had become one of my most trusted companions—always there, full of love, empathy, and cuddles. Especially with Zoey busy with all her extracurriculars and Mom living with Ted, her husband, it often left just Barney and me. He was a great little pup, always wanting to play and, more often, wanting treats. And believe it or not, I'd become quite the sucker for his big brown puppy dog eyes.

Kim replied, "It's so true. I always knew I wanted children, but when I had Audrey, it felt like my universe changed."

"And it probably did."

"Although I still enjoy teaching, and I'm glad Hirsch took the year off. It was nice experiencing all her firsts with him home too."

Kim had taken the school year off after Audrey was born, and Hirsch had taken an extended parental leave so they could experience Audrey's first year as a family. He said it was the only thing that made the job worth it. "How's the nanny working out?" I asked Kim.

The nanny only worked when Kim was teaching, so they used Zoey for after the nanny left for the day. "Oh, she's fantastic. I don't know what we'd do without her and Zoey."

I understood the sentiment. I couldn't imagine raising Zoey without her nanny and then later, my mother.

As we chatted, Hirsch approached. "Having a good time?"

"Of course. Maybe this should be biannual instead of annual," I suggested.

"I'm up for it," Kim chimed in.

Hirsch teased, "Whatever Kim wants, Kim gets. And who am I kidding? Whatever Martina wants, Martina usually gets, too."

It was how I liked it. "We can take turns hosting. I have a back yard and a barbecue, thanks to my mother."

"Did I hear my name?" my mom interjected.

"We were talking about how we should have two barbecues a year, not just one. We can host."

"Of course, you have that grill—it's looking a bit dusty these days."

My mother had inherited all the cooking genes, and it seemed to have skipped a generation down to Zoey. "Well, if you come over and help us barbecue, we could do it," I suggested.

"It's a deal," Mom agreed. "Audrey is so adorable. Every time I see her, she looks more and more like the two of you."

Ted approached us. Hirsch said, "Hey, Sarge."

"It's Ted now, not Sarge. I should call you Sarge." Ted chuckled.

"It hasn't caught on yet. They all still call me Hirsch or boss thanks to Vincent."

"Old habits die hard." Ted shrugged. "How's the job?"

Kim rolled her eyes. "Oh no, here they go."

My mom said, "Let's get out of here before we get sucked into a conversation about Lord only knows what."

They both laughed and hurried away, meeting up with a few other members of the squad who were just coming in. Hirsch said, "Well, it keeps us on our toes."

"Working together again—how's that going?" Ted asked me.

"It's only been a few days, but we're making progress. We'll get these guys and make sure they don't hurt anybody else."

"Like I said, some things never change. I've always admired your confidence and optimism, Martina."

"Thanks, Ted."

Mom could have ended up with a much worse guy, and I was grateful they had found each other. Love in unexpected places.

Unlike Hirsch, my mother had scolded me enough times for me to know to call my new stepfather Ted and not Sarge.

Hirsch interjected. "Okay, enough shop talk. We should

celebrate and mingle with the rest of the squad and their families."

"I guess we have to follow you. You're the boss. *Of the barbecue*, that is."

"I think that's the only thing I'm the boss of these days," he joked back.

As the event got into full swing, there was tons of laughter and smiles. I couldn't imagine a greater bunch of people. Staring out at the crowd from my seat, I watched Zoey creep up with a devilish grin. "Mom, you haven't had a cupcake yet."

What was that look for? "You're right. I'm on my way there now." I rose from my seat and headed toward the dessert table.

Standing next to the display of cupcakes was a man with dark hair and dark eyes. I hadn't seen him before. Was this the setup? Had my daughter sent me over to the cupcake table deliberately to have me meet up with the man? Glancing back at Zoey, I saw she was now huddled with Jayda. They were definitely in cahoots.

Studying my soon-to-be friend, I thought, *not bad*. He was quite handsome. Was I really doing this? I said, "Hi, it looks like you're looking for a sugar fix too."

"Always. It's my weakness," he replied.

"Well, I have a baker living with me. My daughter, Zoey, made the cupcakes."

"Your daughter made these? They look incredible. Is that chocolate caramel?"

"If I recall correctly, it's chocolate cake with sea salt caramel and cream cheese frosting." A heart attack that could fit in the palm of your hand. Throwing caution to the wind, I thought, *One won't kill me.*

"I can hear my doctor telling me I have diabetes now," he joked.

Smiling, I said, "I'm Martina."

"I'm Wilder."

"I'm guessing you're a friend of Jayda's?"

"Guilty as charged."

He was funny. I liked that.

"Sorry. Bad joke. I'm a lawyer. Please don't hold that against me."

"What kind of law do you practice?" I asked.

I found myself surprised at how easy the conversation was. Maybe it was because he was also easy on the eyes, or maybe I had wanted to date for longer than I realized. Or perhaps I just needed it to be something easy or something thrown right in my face.

"I work for the ACLU."

A lawyer for the American Civil Liberties Union, fighting for the rights of the marginalized and those suffering injustices. *Add another point to the yes column.* "I'm guessing you stay pretty busy."

He said, "I do," before picking up a cupcake and placing it on a plate.

I did the same. "Want to join me for a cupcake?"

This, whatever it was, didn't feel strange, like it had the first time I had tried going on a date after Jared had passed. This felt natural. Maybe Hirsch was right. When the time was right, I'd know it. And the time was right.

I brought my plate over to the table where my mom and Ted sat chatting with Ross and his wife, Brynn. I introduced Wilder to the table just as Jayda walked up. "Hi, everyone. Oh my, look at those cupcakes. I'll be right back." She gave me a meaningful look before scurrying away. *Oh, Jayda.*

As we sat down, Ross said, "So, what do you do, Wilder?"

After he explained, I asked, "Where are you from?"

"Bay Area, born and raised," he replied.

"No kidding?"

"Nope, you?"

"Same. Grew up on Stone Island, and now I live in the East Bay. Working at my firm, Drakos Monroe Security & Investigations."

"You're a partner?"

"I took on the role about five years ago after the sheriff's department kicked me out," I said with a chuckle.

Ted smirked. "That's one way to put it."

Teasing, I said, "Ted was our sergeant. He's the one who told me, 'Get out, lady.'"

My mother tsked. "Oh, Martina, you can be so bad sometimes. He did not say that. It was budget cuts."

I shrugged. "Tomato, *tomahto*."

Wilder smiled at me, and he had a dazzling white smile. My gosh, I thought I was developing a crush. Was that what this feeling was? That tingling in my gut wasn't a warning there was a bad guy in the midst, but actual romantic feelings? Or at least an interest in romantic feelings? This was new and kind of exciting.

I picked up my fork, skimmed the frosting off the top of my cupcake, and took a bite. It was pure sugar and butter and utterly incredible. "This is amazing."

"Well, I'm behind. I better have some of that," he replied, picking up his cupcake, peeling back the paper, and taking a big bite. "Your daughter made this?"

"She did," I said with a smile.

Mom said, "Zoey's quite the baker. But I think she likes to bake because she gets to put sprinkles on everything. She's loved glitter since I've known her."

"She still loves glitter, and she's sixteen." And I hoped that never changed.

He leaned back and placed his hand on his chest, as if he

was surprised. "You have a sixteen-year-old daughter? You don't look a day over twenty-five."

I thought, *well, he's definitely flirting with me because I certainly look more than a day over twenty-five. More like fifteen years over twenty-five.* But, I admit, I appreciated the compliment. And didn't think I could remember the last time I'd received one. "You're sweet."

My mom turned to Ted and said, "Are you thirsty? There's iced tea."

Ted studied Wilder and me. "I am very thirsty," he said, not so subtly.

I had always been fond of Ted when we worked together, but since he'd been with my mom, I liked him even more. He was so good to her, so sweet and attentive. They were a great couple. It seemed everybody had paired up. Was I sitting next to half of my new couple? Or was I totally jumping the gun? Was I so out of practice I didn't know how to do this? Well, if that was true, I guessed I'd just have to go with my gut, like I always did.

Soon the others at the table made excuses, and it was just Wilder and me who remained. He looked at me and said, "Everybody knows Jayda is trying to set us up, right?"

I laughed and said, "I think so."

"I have to admit, I'm not sorry about that."

"And I'm glad Jayda overstepped."

He laughed heartily, and I liked it. He was funny and understood my humor. Not to mention he was very easy on the eyes.

He said, "Jayda has a way of being a bit of a bulldozer. But she's great."

"How do you know her?" I asked.

"Went to college with her husband, Rory."

"Okay, it's all making sense now." Was I smiling?

"I hope I'm not being too forward, but I'd love to take you to dinner sometime?"

My gosh, I was being asked on a date, and I was happy to say yes. "I'd like that." We exchanged phone numbers into each other's cell phones. *Dating is so different now.* As he was handing my phone back to me, he said, "Oh, I think you're getting a call."

Glancing at the screen, I said, "I'm so sorry. I need to take this."

"No worries. Please do."

I turned away and said, "Hello?"

"This is Daphne, Katie Kimble's friend. We talked last week."

My pulse quickened. "Did you remember something?"

"I just got a call from Katie."

Wait, what? "Are you sure it was her?"

"I think so."

That was certainly unexpected. "Did she say where she was, if she was safe?"

"All she said was she was okay, but before I could ask her where she was, the call ended."

Katie was alive, and I was going on a date? I thanked Daphne, told her I'd be in touch, and hung up the phone.

Wilder said, "Is that about your case?"

Katie was alive? "Yes, it's a huge development, actually."

"I'm guessing you need to run." Before I could say anything, he said, "It's okay. I have your number, and you've agreed to dinner. I'm going to hold you to that."

No arguments here. After a quick, silent prayer, I said, "I'm looking forward to dinner," before saying goodbye and rushing over to Vincent and Hirsch to tell them the news.

29

———

FERN

I FELT like a bird in a cage. Atlas was my captor, albeit a somewhat charming one. At least he had been since moving me from the warehouse. But he had insisted on keeping me confined within the motel room, under the pretense of love and concern for my safety. Each passing day was a test of my endurance, my ability to gain his trust again, and my determination to escape this criminal life that had gone *way too far*.

In the last two days, I had convinced Atlas of our reconciliation and that I was entirely on board with him, whatever that meant. Because he hadn't confided in me his plans or why we were hiding out.

The constant façade was draining, eroding my spirit, a harsh reminder of the real me I had to hide. His actions, like going out to fetch breakfast while leaving me behind, were a testament to his indifference to his safety as opposed to mine or his lack of trust in me. His plans for us remained vague, and I was growing restless within the motel's noisy confines.

Atlas said, "There's something I want to talk to you about."

I stared up into his eyes and said, "Okay." Was he finally going to tell me what was going on?

"The head thinks the Bay Area operation is compromised, and his associates aren't very happy about it. And not happy with me. Or you. They think you can't be trusted."

That didn't bode well for me. "What did you tell him?"

"That I had it under control."

The operation *and me*. "Did he believe you?"

Atlas furrowed his brow. "I don't know. I think we should lay low for a bit. Go to Mexico. Until all of this blows over."

"To Mexico?" It was hard to hide my surprise. I'd never heard Atlas talk about Mexico or wanting to go there. What on earth would we do in Mexico? Remembering I needed to be supportive and on board, I said, "How long would we be gone?"

"I don't know. Maybe for good. It depends. But it'll be you and me together. We can spend the rest of our days hanging on the beach."

"Really?" Like, really?

"Yes, really. I think it's the only way."

"And the head won't come after us?"

"No, not the head. But there's more to worry about than the head. I think he still trusts me. He knows I would never talk to the police, and I know you wouldn't either. He was concerned because he doesn't know you as well as he knows me. And that's when I told him I would go away for a bit. I didn't tell him where. That's why I've had to keep you in here, my darling. I'm sorry I wasn't more honest before."

He was keeping me prisoner. He didn't care about my safety like I thought he had.

"You know how much I love you, Fern. We'll have a whole new life in Mexico. It'll be great, I promise."

"And it's the only way?"

"It's the only way to stay safe. For both of us."

"When do we leave?"

"Soon. I'm still putting together some details to make sure we have a place to stay and our new identities."

He seemed to know an awful lot about how to disappear. "Have you done this before?"

His eyes met mine, and he said, "We don't need to get into that now. But let's just say I know how to go off the grid where nobody can trace me, and you'll learn to do the same. It's all going to work out. It's going to be like everything we ever talked about. Tranquility, harmony... but it can't be here anymore."

I gave him a reassuring smile and said, "Okay, let's go. I trust you." I wrapped my arms around him before we shared a passionate kiss.

The first time he promised me the world, I believed him. But I was no longer that stupid. I only hoped he believed every word. And that I could figure out how to break free of him before he whisked me off to Mexico, where I knew I would never be free again.

30

MARTINA

THE CORNERS of my mouth curled upward as I lifted the lid of my laptop.

"Why are you looking so happy this morning? Were they able to trace the call from Katie to Daphne?"

Distracted, I hadn't heard Hirsch walk in. With a bemused smile, he sat next to me and placed his coffee cup on the table. "No. The call came from a burner phone. Unless she calls again from a landline, we're out of luck." I paused, and said, "Was I smiling?"

"You were."

Not sure if I should share, I took a chance. "Well, I have a crush, Hirsch."

He sat back and looked at me. "A crush on Wilder, Jayda's friend?"

My head bopped up and down. "He just texted me to finalize our dinner plans. We're going out Saturday night."

"Well, then we better wrap up this case before that."

Trying not to smile like a goof, I couldn't believe I had feelings about someone, even if it was just beginning. And who knows, it could turn out to be nothing, but at least it would get me out there. It made me see I wanted a relationship. "Fingers crossed."

"But seriously, I think it's great. He seems nice, and I saw the way he looked at you. He was quite taken with you."

My cheeks burned.

"How does it feel being on the other end?" Hirsch asked.

Had I teased him a lot when we he first started dating Kim? It was so long ago, I couldn't remember, but I probably had. "It's fine. I'm looking forward to going out with him, and that's kind of strange, right?"

"It means you're ready, Martina. You could go out twice, twenty times, or you may never see him after the first date. Or... you could end up at the altar. Who knows? But you're making a great first step. I can see it on your face. This is right for you."

Not completely comfortable with the conversation about my personal feelings and romance, I said, "Okay, enough about that. Let's get to work. Where's everybody?"

We were about to embark on a marathon surveillance footage viewing party. Our team at Drakos Monroe had set up the drones over the Jenner property and saved the footage for us to check out. They flagged a few spots for us to pay special attention to.

Jayda and Ross strolled in. "Happy Sunday, y'all," Ross said in a monotone voice.

Hirsch said, "You could have taken the day off if you wanted."

"I'm teasing. Happy to be here. Good to see your smiling faces."

Jayda punched Ross in the arm. "Be nice."

"I'm always nice," Ross retorted. "Where's Vincent?"

"He'll be here in a couple of minutes. He stopped at the drive-through to get something for breakfast." Checking my wrist, I said, "Make that brunch."

Hirsch said, "You're letting him eat fast food?"

"He's young. He does what he wants."

"He's becoming more and more like you," Ross said.

I gave a fake scowl. It was good to be back. Jayda sat at the table next to me. "A little birdie told me you have dinner plans Saturday night."

"It's true, and thank you. He's nice."

"You're very welcome. I'm thinking positive thoughts for you."

We truly were a family—one that teased, one that encouraged, one that set us up with romantic prospects when we didn't ask for it.

Vincent walked in, a french fry hanging out of his mouth. He finished swallowing it and said, "Let's get this done. Let's find Katie and take down the bad guys. I'm ready. Are you ready? Are you pumped?"

"I'd be more ready if I could have some of whatever you had." Not that I partook in anything illegal, being eight years sober and all.

"Enthusiasm, charm—it's all for the taking," he said in a theatrical tone.

He sat down and popped another fry in his mouth. "Okay, where are we at?"

Hirsch said, "We'll check in with the Sonoma County Sheriff's Department to get a report on the warehouse."

"Let's do it."

Hirsch smirked. I could tell he was amused by Vincent. He dialed, and we listened to the Polycom. "This is Sergeant Hirsch from CoCo County."

"Hey, Hirsch. It's Detective Birdie."

"I'm here with the rest of the team: Ross, Jayda, Vincent, and Martina. Got any news for us?"

"It's been a quiet weekend. We've done round-the-clock

surveillance of the warehouse. There's no cars or signs of anybody going in or out."

"They must have abandoned it," Hirsch said to me. "Maybe they spotted us or heard us or something spooked them."

Detective Birdie responded, "That could be. Let us know if you need our help with anything else. We'll keep watching unless you want us to stop."

"Keep watching."

"You got it. We'll keep you updated."

"Thank you." Hirsch leaned back. "Sounds like Atlas and his crew have abandoned the warehouse."

"But it's only been a few days. We don't know what their cadence is for visiting the site. They could only go once a week or once every couple of days. Sonoma County needs to keep monitoring them."

"Agreed."

With the team nodding heads in agreement, I took it as a sign it was time to move on to the drone footage and connected my laptop to the projector. It whirred to life, and I said, "There's a lot to cover. We'll start with the footage our surveillance team flagged for us. Unless you all want to start at the beginning of the entire twenty-four hours of video?"

Ross said, "I think I speak for all of us when I say, let's start with the flagged videos."

Vincent cocked his head. "Are you sure? I could narrate."

Chuckling, I said, "Starting with the flagged video it is." Tapping away, I found the files in my email and pulled up the first clip.

"That looks like the entrance to the farm," Vincent said.

"That's because it is." We sat watching, waiting, and seeing nothing. After a minute, I said, "The head of the drone team sent a note for this one. They positioned this drone on the entrance the entire time. Nobody entered or exited since Saturday morning."

"Which means Atlas could be there or not."

We hadn't seen Atlas in three days. Which meant he could be anywhere. And knowing that Katie was alive made me want to talk to Atlas more than ever. I had half a mind to get in my car and drive to Jenner right now, demand to talk to Atlas once again. Moving to the next flagged clip, I clicked play. A still shot of two figures appeared on the screen.

"Who are those two?" Ross asked.

The clarity of the video was remarkable. "That's Sage and Cloud."

"What do you think they're doing?"

The two figures were walking on the road. The drone followed them. When they looked up and possibly spotted the drone, Sage and Cloud strolled under some trees and were no longer visible. They could have been out for a walk or hike. The footage showed having a commune in Jenner would be a brilliant cover. A lot of natural hiding places, and your enemies would be easy to spot.

A grove of trees appeared on the screen before the drone zoomed lower, closer to the ground. I froze the video. "What does that look like?"

"Looks like a grave," Jayda said.

My gaze shifted to Hirsch. "What do you think?"

"I agree with Jayda. Looks like a grave, freshly dug, a few weeks tops."

Were we too late? If the woman from the warehouse was in the grave, should we have risked everything to save her? Was her death on our hands?

Hirsch said, "I'm glad you decided against going undercover. If they're burying bodies on the property, I don't think they'd hesitate to put you underground."

Noted. "Let's check the other videos." I opened the next video file and said, "There's a decent shot of their crops. Let's see what the team flagged here." On the screen, there were a few rows of lush green plants with clusters of buds on their distinctive crowns. "Marijuana plants. These we knew about."

"Likely just recreational. That's not enough to be selling it, right?" Ross asked.

Hirsch said, "I wouldn't think so."

"We were on the property. It definitely smelled like people were using it recreationally."

A few snickers emitted from the team.

"They're certainly not as concerning as a grave." We sat through a few more marked videos. I couldn't help but think about the grave or potential grave. Was it the woman we didn't save? And where the heck was Atlas? I sat quietly as the team discussed different scenarios for how to continue. We had lost our drug dealers. We had lost Atlas. And there was no sign of Katie.

"We should put out a BOLO on Atlas's car. The fact that we're clueless about his location is unsettling to me."

Hirsch said, "We can do that."

"We need to question him about Katie's whereabouts. If she's still alive, he may know where she's at. Not to mention he's a suspect in the drug operation." Not only alive, but in danger. Based on Daphne's description of the phone call, it could have been cut short because Katie didn't want who she was with to hear the conversation.

"We'll get it done."

I fixed my gaze on the screen, devoid of any signs of Atlas and Katie. Where were they?

31

HIRSCH

As I ENTERED the task force conference room, I couldn't help but feel a noticeable spring in my step. I felt alive. More than alive; I felt electrified. It wasn't a secret I missed solving cases, but it wasn't until now I understood how much.

I loved my life with Audrey and Kim. It was more than I ever dreamed of, but there was the other part of me that loved the action, the adrenaline rush, and being part of a team solving tough mysteries. It's what I was meant to do, and I couldn't just put it in a desk drawer and forget about it while I played with the brass all day.

There was a paradoxical emotion within me. I was eager to solve the case, but I was a little sad for it to end. Because once the case was solved, the task force would disband, and I would be back behind the desk. At least until the next big case.

For the morale of the team, I had to stay upbeat. Sure, we would solve this case, but it certainly wouldn't be the last tough one. Humanity was capable of so many atrocities, and the world needed our team to bring justice to victims and their families. That wouldn't change. If it did, I'd be more than happy to be out of a job, spending my days barbecuing and playing with my daughter in the back yard. We could even adopt a dog or two.

Boy, did Audrey love Barney. My mind drifted to the barbecue. The way her eyes lit up when she threw the ball and watched Barney sprint across the lawn warmed my heart. Kim and I agreed, we didn't have the capacity for another living creature to take care of, especially if we were to add another human to the mix one day. We would have to be content with visits from Barney and his owners, Zoey and Martina.

Inside the task force room, Martina and Vincent were already chattering away, standing near the whiteboard. It was like old times, except we had Vincent full time as an investigator. I'd known investigations would be a good fit for him and was glad he found his footing at Drakos Monroe. Working alongside Martina, he could hone his skills and become the best version of Vincent Teller, PI, he could be. It had been incredible to watch him over the years, and I knew we could rely on him.

"Hey," I greeted them.

"Morning, Sarge," Vincent replied in a teasing tone. He was obviously amused by his new moniker for me. He'd already gotten everyone calling me "boss," and now he was going to get the "Sarge" thing rolling too. I didn't know if I would ever get used to it.

Martina gave me a playful wink, and said, "Morning, Sarge."

Things were a lot sillier around the office with those two around. "Just got a call from the DEA. They said they can come down to meet us."

"Do they have any leads for us?" Martina asked.

"We won't know until they come in. Last week, I sent over surveillance photos, along with a brief on everything we have learned about Atlas, the Sunny D deaths, and Katie Kimble. I don't think the drone footage will help them, but we can share it when they get here. Hopefully, we can ID some players we saw interacting with Atlas outside the warehouse. We need to know who these people are and how dangerous they are."

"Agreed."

"What are you working on over there?" I asked.

"You know how we love a good murder board?" Vincent replied.

Memories drifted to previous cases, each of us standing near the board coming up with theories and connecting dots. "I do."

"We have all the Sunny D victims' names: Martha, Jennifer, Samual, Yearly, and Terrence. We have the names of all the known dealers: Zander, who connects to Ashworth, who connects to Atlas, connected to these three unknown persons pictured. These are still shots from the videos and surveillance photos taken outside the warehouse. Over here, we have all our suspect locations. We have the commune in Jenner, we've got the warehouse in Santa Rosa, but now we have a question mark. Because we don't know where they are."

"Hopefully that changes," I said. "At least nobody else has died that we know of."

"Small favors," Martina commented. "What time is the DEA getting here?"

"In thirty minutes. Let's grab Jayda and Ross. I want them here when we speak to them."

"Good thinking."

After a few calls, we waited for the rest of the team and brainstormed theories about Katie Kimble and where she could be and how she fit into all of it. We knew she was dating Atlas, but if she was with him the last two years, why not tell us? Why the secrecy? A lot of things about this case didn't make sense, but I was confident we would figure it out.

AFTER INTRODUCTIONS, DEA agents Bishop and Sampson said, "We've heard about you, Martina and Hirsch. You're all from the Cold Case Squad, right?"

Martina winked at me. "That's right. Now we're working on a special task force to figure out who is behind the Sunny D deaths and our missing person, Katie Kimble."

"Well, you two have quite a reputation for stepping into all kinds of jurisdictions."

Martina put her hands up in defense. "Not on purpose. We go where the case leads us."

Agent Bishop leaned back. "No offense meant. That shows good detective work. Now, what we're about to share with you is extremely confidential. Based on your reputation, what we hear around the DEA, and the backgrounds of all your investigators, we think we can trust you."

The five of us from the sheriff's department and Drakos Monroe looked at each other and exchanged nods. "We understand confidentiality."

"Excellent. Then I think we'll work great together."

"Why so secretive?" Vincent asked. He wasn't an investigator when we had worked with the DEA before. They had been useful in our pursuit of a missing person who was connected to organized crime, namely baby and drug trafficking.

Agent Bishop said, "We have active investigations that could be compromised if local law enforcement gets involved, i.e., the people in this room. If you take down some of our mid-level members, even some of the low-levels, it could ruin the entire operation."

Vincent grew serious. "Got it."

"Do you have a projector?" Agent Sampson asked. Then he stopped. "Actually, it looks like you've got them up on the board over there."

"Yes," I confirmed as the agent swaggered over to the whiteboard.

"I will not write down the names. As I mentioned, this is confidential. We've passed around the photos, and we're fairly certain of three of the identities. One is uncertain. I'm having some of my colleagues in Southern California look into him." He pointed to the picture of Atlas. "This is the one we're unsure about. He looks kinda familiar, but we're not a hundred percent certain. It's hard to tell with the facial hair."

"Understood," Martina said.

"This guy here, he's a bad dude. Raphael Peña, born and raised in Los Angeles. He's tatted up pretty good from a street gang he was a part of that was fond of trafficking drugs from Mexico. The second guy here, with the dark hair and dark eyes, is Kenneth Martin, from Newport Beach. He's high in the organization, as is Jacob Briggs, over here. He's likely the top dog. A Malibu surfer turned drug trafficker."

Glancing around the room, I saw that the team was speechless. "So, these three are part of a drug trafficking organization from Southern California?"

Agent Bishop said, "Oh, yeah, they're part of a very large international organization. We think Briggs started it all. Not to say he was the first to be dealing, but in addition to a drug smuggler, he styles himself as an enlightenment guru."

"An enlightenment guru turned drug trafficker?" Vincent asked incredulously.

"These guys think they're the second coming of the Brotherhood of Eternal Love, a commune from the 1960s that was inspired by Timothy Leary from Harvard and his experimental work with LSD. The Brotherhood thought by giving everybody LSD, they'd see the truth and become enlightened, leading to a utopian world. But then they got mixed up with some dealers and thought smuggling hashish from Afghanistan was the perfect complement to their lifestyle." Agent Bishop snorted, a sardonic grin spreading across his face. "Ridiculous. Anyway, we think Briggs and Martin started with the same idea, and initially they only dealt with LSD. Apparently, they didn't fancy trekking over to the now-war-torn middle east for hashish."

"How did that evolve into drug trafficking?" I asked.

"Well, you see, Jacob Briggs and his pal Kenneth Martin got greedy. They built this beautiful property down in Southern California and enjoyed the good life, and they liked young women. They were pretty small-time—making their own LSD, handing it out at concerts—but then Briggs met Rafael Peña. Rafael showed them a path to a load of cash. Briggs liked what he saw, and the trio joined forces, starting to smuggle in fentanyl from Mexico."

Wild.

"And you don't know how our guy Atlas fits in?" Martina asked.

"We're looking into it," he replied.

Martina asked, "What about the warehouse?"

"The team working the case has suspected the trio wanted to expand production, and the Bay Area makes sense. We think that's why Atlas rented the warehouse."

"What about human trafficking? If they're into young women, could it be possible they would've kidnapped our missing person, Katie Kimble, for their own entertainment or to sell?"

"It's not really their style. They have enough drugs and money to get women without having to take them by force, but I wouldn't put it past them. For a long time, they were pretty peaceful, until they teamed up with Rafael Peña. He's got a dark side, and it spread to both Martin and Briggs."

With the understanding that Atlas's associates were based

in Southern California, I wondered if that was where he'd fled to. If he had Katie, was she there too? "Sounds like you have an ongoing operation you don't want us to mess up," I observed.

"That's correct," Agent Bishop confirmed.

"What are we supposed to do? Just wait to see if you find Katie?" Martina asked, frustration seeping into her tone.

"We can't have law enforcement approaching any of the members. They call themselves the Brothers. Original, right?" Agent Bishop's voice dripped with sarcasm.

"What about PIs just simply looking for a missing person?" Martina asked.

Our eyes met; I knew exactly what she was thinking.

"A PI looking for a missing person may be okay," Agent Bishop conceded.

Martina said, "We've approached him before; he says he doesn't know where she is. But with our new information, we believe she's alive and he knows where she is. I don't buy his story. Especially now."

"Since you've already made contact, I would say you could follow the missing person angle, but no mention of the drugs. My team is really close to bringing them down. A confidential informant told us you have one of the low-level dealers in custody. It's got them nervous. Nervous drug dealers with violent tendencies are not a good situation. So, if you do approach Atlas, and if he's part of the organization, proceed with extreme caution. Extreme."

Before we said our goodbyes, we transferred samples of Sunny D for the DEA labs to compare to known drugs being distributed by the Brothers. If there was a match, we'd have our killers. But what could we do? We couldn't go in and arrest them without jeopardizing the DEA's operation.

Martina gave a slight head tilt, and I hoped it meant she

understood we needed to ensure she, Vincent, and anyone else she brought into the case were safe.

We thanked the agents for coming in. They assured us they would call as soon as they learned the identity of Atlas. Who was he? Where was he? And did he have Katie? I was thankful we had reached out to the DEA. Who knows what we would've stepped into if we hadn't? Organized crime was a whole different animal. A very complicated and dangerous animal.

32

———

MARTINA

WHILE SLIPPING INTO MY BACKPACK, I greeted Hirsch with a wave. "They've got a location on Atlas's car. We're about to go check it out."

"Hold on. I just heard back from the DEA, and you'll want to hear what they had to say."

We were about to find out who Atlas really was. This ought to be interesting.

"They know who he is?" Vincent asked.

"They do. Are you ready for this?"

My heart rate sped up. "Ready."

Vincent echoed my sentiment.

"Thirty-five years ago, Ryan Harris, aka Atlas, was born in London, England."

"A Brit?" Vincent asked.

"Indeed. And not a law-abiding one. Before he immigrated illegally to the United States, and likely purchased a new identity, he was a well-known drug dealer in Europe. And when I say drug dealer, I mean trafficker accused of multiple offenses, including murder. The DEA suspects he worked with his old smuggling pals to set him up in the U.S. But law enforcement lost sight of him over the last ten years and assumed he was dead until now."

He'd been living under an assumed name on a commune, hiding from the authorities. My gut had been spot on during the initial interview with Katie's parents—the case was dangerous.

Hirsch added, "He's on Interpol's most wanted."

Shaking my head in disbelief, I said, "He's been hiding out in the U.S., building this community of earth lovers, but it's all been a ruse to evade law enforcement?"

"And dealing." Hirsch smirked. "They're pretty happy about finding him."

I would think so. "Does that mean I can't approach him and ask about Katie?"

"Agent Bishop says you can talk to him about Katie, but don't spook him—no mention of his true identity or the drugs or the warehouse."

"I can handle that. Can you, Vincent?"

Vincent bobbed his head dramatically. "Consider it handled."

"You want backup?" Hirsch asked.

"We'd appreciate it. Our plan is to park a couple of blocks away and inspect the vehicle and the area on foot. The car's parked outside a motel. Our plan is to catch him when he's in the parking lot."

"All right. I'll request a couple of patrol officers, and we'll head over. We'll lie low until we hear from you."

"Sounds like a plan." I couldn't help but smile. It was just like the old days, the rush of working with incredible investigators and a team who went above and beyond to help each other. There were no big egos or wanting the credit all for themselves. Each one of them was all in to solve the case. It was an incredible feeling—like being a part of something great.

VINCENT STAYED several paces back as I approached the motel parking lot, not wanting to look suspicious, even though Atlas—or should I say, Ryan Harris—knew who we were. Still reeling from the realization he was an international drug dealer hiding out in the US was mind-boggling. For a half a second, I'd thought maybe he actually was a man who wanted peace and to live off the land. He was quite the actor and was likely a master manipulator. If life was a movie, the Academy Awards would be calling him any day.

Strolling past his blue SUV, I confirmed the license plate number and continued on. I walked around the block, returned to some hedges, and took cover. Vincent followed. The two of us crouched down behind the bushes, and I said, "I have confirmation on the vehicle."

"Confirmed," Vincent echoed.

"Now we wait."

"That's right."

"Do you think anyone will drive by and think it's weird we're huddled behind some bushes?"

As my gaze wandered, I became aware there were a steady stream of people on the street, and cars frequently drove past. Although we were not easily visible, Vincent had a valid point. "Maybe we should move the car to the parking lot. He knows who we are. He knows I'm a private investigator looking for Katie. So, maybe we don't need to be quite so clandestine."

"It'll look more natural."

In my excitement, I hadn't considered that. That and it could take several hours before he actually came out for us to talk to him. We headed back to the car, drove into the lot, and parked in a stall across from Atlas's vehicle. Visibility was good, and we wouldn't stick out like a sore thumb.

Inside the car, I called Hirsch. "We're in the car, waiting for him to come out. We have confirmation it's his car."

"Okay, keep us updated. Units are here. We're two blocks over."

"Sure thing."

Vincent said, "Should we take bets on how long it's going to take for him to come out?"

"I can't bet. I'm in AA."

He laughed. "True, true. How's your sponsee doing?"

"She's struggling, and she calls me every day which I think is helping her. I'm glad I signed up to be a sponsor."

"That's so cool. And your mom's a sponsor too, right?"

"She is. She's been doing it a lot longer than I have. It's nice to give back, you know. I practically owe my entire life to my sponsor."

"I can't imagine you as an alcoholic."

"Well, I am an alcoholic—a recovering alcoholic. And as you may not be surprised to hear, when I was drinking, I hid it and continued to try to do my job. It wasn't until I got into a near-fatal accident, and my boss came into my hospital room and told me to get my act together or I was out a job, that I realized how much I'd fallen from grace. And that I couldn't handle it all on my own."

"That's incredible, Martina."

Keeping my eyes on the SUV, I said, "Did you have a conversation with Amanda?"

"I did."

"And?"

"She says she's okay with waiting for kids."

"See, communication is key."

"Yeah, and I'm kind of thinking about asking her a pretty big question."

Without thinking, I turned away from the car and stared at Vincent with raised brows. "Really?"

He blushed. "Really. Like I said, she's my person. I want to experience everything, and I want her to be right next to me experiencing it too."

"That's wonderful."

"Hey." He pointed.

Wrapped up in Vincent's love life, I almost missed Atlas. "Let's go."

We hopped out of the car and jogged toward Atlas. He was still wearing his linen pants and cotton T-shirt, his hair flowing in the wind. Wearing sunglasses, his face was barely visible between the bushy beard and dark lenses. I waved, and he grimaced. "Atlas."

"Miss Monroe. What a surprise."

Reaching him at his car door, I said, "You remember my partner, Vincent?"

"I do. Good to see you, Vincent. I'm guessing this isn't a coincidence?"

"It's not. As you know, I'm a private investigator, as is Vincent, and we're looking for Katie. We have reason to believe she is alive." I wished he wasn't wearing his sunglasses so I could gauge his expression. It was like talking to a wall.

"That's great news."

"You haven't heard from her?"

"I haven't heard from Katie in two years."

"And nobody's come looking for her until us?"

"Nobody."

Despite not being able to see his facial expression, knowing what I knew about Ryan Harris, I didn't buy his act. Fists on hips, I said, "Atlas, I know you don't know me very well, but I have this thing where when I have a case, I don't stop investigating until I solve it."

Vincent said, "I can attest to that. She's like a dog with a bone."

Atlas removed his sunglasses and stared deep into my eyes, inching closer. "I'm pleading with you to drop it."

I puffed out my chest and said, "Are you threatening me?"

"It's not me you have to worry about. There are far worse people than me to be afraid of."

Processing his words, I said, "Like who?"

"Miss Monroe, please drop it. Or you will be sorry."

"I don't take kindly to threats."

"They will come after you. That's a promise. Now, if you care about your life and your partner's, you'll let it go. Don't contact me again."

It was clear Atlas was scared, not of me, but of who he was working with.

"Thank you for your time, Atlas." I glanced at Vincent, and we both went back to the car.

As we drove out of the parking lot, I used my hands-free device to call Hirsch. "Hey, you're on speaker."

"How did it go?"

"He denies knowing where she is. But get this—he told us to stop looking for Katie or our lives will be in danger."

"Do you think it's a credible threat?"

"He seemed nervous, not just for us, but for himself."

"If the Brothers think he has PIs or even worse, law enforcement sniffing around, his pals may think he's a snitch and come after him. And if he's got Katie, it could put her life in danger too. Maybe we back off for now, come up with another plan."

"All right. We'll meet you back at the station."

"Be safe, Martina. You too, Vincent."

Vincent called out, "Thanks, Sarge."

Hirsch sighed.

With a chuckle, I said, "See you soon, Sarge."

As I ended the call with a smile, I said, "Looks like we stepped into a whopper of a case."

Vincent grinned. "You love it."

True. And with a promise to keep, I wouldn't quit until I found Katie.

33

———

FERN

THE JINGLE of the key in the lock made me freeze momentarily before I moved my hand down by my side and rushed over to sit on the edge of the bed. "You're back?" I asked, my voice barely above a whisper.

He told me he was grabbing lunch. Why had he come back so quickly? Had he suspected I was planning an escape?

"We have a situation," he announced, a grave look on his face.

"A situation?" The words sent an icy shiver down my spine. *He knows.* Was he going to kill me?

"The people who came to the community looking for Katie —they followed me here and just approached me in the parking lot. They said they won't stop until they find her."

"Do they know about the business?"

"I don't know. But I don't like them following me. It's a bad sign. And if the head finds out, he could think I'm talking to the cops. You know what they'll do to me."

With a nod, I acknowledged I knew exactly what they would do. Atlas was already on edge, and I was trying my best to conceal the fact I was a nervous wreck, but I was worried.

Although Atlas seemed like less of a threat, the Brothers were a different story. They didn't care who they hurt, as long as they were safe. Atlas explained as much, but I could tell by the look in their eyes each time we met they were out for themselves, despite their spewing on about enlightenment and the greater good.

It was the same nonsense Atlas had preached to all of his community—his followers, his minions. I didn't realize I was just like them, a sheep following blindly, doing his dirty work for him. I still couldn't believe what I had gotten myself into.

"What are you going to do?" I asked, trying to sound calm.

He seemed to ponder my question. Would he kill the private investigators to keep them from coming back? That seemed pretty risky and kind of rash.

"I don't know. Can't have them following me, coming around. What if they go to the cops?"

"We have to do what we have to do, right?"

"What does that mean?"

I meant to be reassuring, but perhaps that wasn't how it came off. "If we need to get out of town or take care of things, it's what we should do. Anything you want, Atlas. Let's get it done," I said, trying to sound encouraging.

Inside, I was shaking like a leaf, but on the outside, I was doing my best to slow my breathing, fearing my nerves would get the better of me. He began pacing around the motel room, and I suggested, "Maybe we should get something to eat. That will help us think clearly, come up with the right plan."

I hoped he understood it was *our* plan. I was with him, even though the first chance I got, I was running. He stopped and stared at me, his eyes hard and unyielding.

"I suppose a simple solution is to give them what they want."

"What they want?"

"They want Katie. They want to know where she is."

He wouldn't do that, would he? "What does that mean? Would the Brothers get upset?"

"If Katie is dead, Katie can't talk."

Atlas's eyes were dark and brooding.

Fear took hold of me. "You can't be serious."

"I don't know. Just thinking of all the different scenarios."

"I love you, Atlas. I won't do anything to hurt you."

He gave me a look that made me think I hadn't been as convincing as I hoped. "We need to think of a plan to get out of here. Our best bet is Mexico. If we're there, nobody will look for us."

"I love the beach."

He pulled me in and squeezed me tight, almost too tight. I didn't believe, not even for a moment, that he wouldn't hurt me. This trip to Mexico could be a ruse. In reality, I could be following him straight to my grave.

34

—————

MARTINA

On a call with the DEA, I explained the conversation I had with Atlas outside the motel room.

Agent Bishop said, "It sounds like he's scared, which means he's likely to run."

"The Brothers would take him out for talking to a private investigator about Katie Kimble?" I asked.

"Well, according to the CI, they think their Bay Area operation may be in jeopardy. If they blame him, then sure," he replied.

Sitting across from Hirsch, I gave him a look to take it over.

"How do you want us to proceed?" Hirsch asked.

"Stay away from Atlas. However, if you have the resources to spare, we could use your help on the case."

Hirsch said, "We have patrol on Atlas at all times."

"The DEA would be mighty grateful if you keep eyes on him and let us know if it looks like he's going to run," Agent Bishop said.

"We can do that."

"Great. But I have to reiterate, stay away from Atlas aka Ryan Harris. Don't approach him. We don't want it to look like he's talking to the police. It's best to keep him alive. He likely knows a lot. Plus, Interpol wants him bad. We'd really like to see this guy in custody, thrown in jail, and locked away forever."

"Understood," I said. "What about Katie Kimble?"

"We don't know," Agent Bishop admitted. "What are you thinking?"

"Well, there's another guy just below Atlas, Ashworth Dante. He may have seen Katie. We could go at him."

"He could run it up to Atlas and tell him what's going on," Agent Bishop warned.

I bristled slightly at his caution. "What if I was undercover? Ashworth doesn't know me. With a wig and glasses, I could pretend to be Katie's mother looking for her. I could hit Ashworth's known stomping grounds, position myself on the sidewalk with flyers of Katie asking if anyone has seen her. When I bump into Ashworth, I'll do the same." I could only imagine what it would be like to have to stop strangers on the street to ask if they'd seen Zoey. The idea was unsettling. "As long as I don't blow my cover, it shouldn't be an issue."

"That should be fine. Anything else you want us to know? We'll keep in touch and let you know if anything develops on our side. And you'll keep us informed if there are any developments with Atlas or if you learn anything new from Ashworth Dante."

"Okay, we'll keep in touch," I confirmed, ending the call.

Hirsch turned off the Polycom and looked out at Jayda, Ross, Vincent, and me.

"Sounds like the DEA wants us to back off and do the grunt work for them, watching Atlas. What about our case?" Ross asked.

"You're right, and I don't enjoy being put in the back seat to watch Atlas and do nothing. But the DEA and us—we have a common goal, let's not forget that. Sometimes in this job, we have to exercise a bit of patience, right Martina?"

He had a way of singling me out when he wanted to emphasize a point. "Why are you looking at me, Hirsch?"

"No reason," he replied.

With a slight shake of my head, I said, "Anyway, I have an undercover operation to plan out. I'm going to need backup. Vincent, you in?"

"I'm always in."

"How about the rest of you? Would you be interested?" I asked the team.

"Do you think you'll need backup talking to Ashworth?" Hirsch asked.

"Based on his background check, it seems like he's pretty low level. No criminal record and not much of a threat. But better safe than sorry."

"What about a wire? Could be useful if he talks about Atlas," Hirsch suggested.

It was a bit optimistic and a little overboard, but it wouldn't hurt anything. "Hook me up."

"All right, let's plan on having a surveillance team with you when you approach Ashworth. You never know how things might go down. We think he's low level, but that doesn't mean the Brothers aren't looking out for him, maybe even watching him," Hirsch cautioned.

Hirsch took his responsibilities as the boss seriously. His caution never hurt us before, and I didn't think it would now. "It's a plan. Let's get to it."

With that, I was about to go on my first undercover mission in several years but had no doubt I could pull it off. It was like riding a bike, right?

35

———

MARTINA

Fitted with a blonde wig, dark-framed spectacles, and a wire, I clutched a stack of flyers with Katie Kimble's picture on them as well as her descriptors and the date she went missing. It had been forever since I'd been undercover, but I knew how to use my emotions to be believable. I had to pretend the flyers I was clutching in my arms had a picture of Zoey, my daughter's face, and not somebody I'd never met before.

Although I wasn't sure how much strength I would have if I hadn't seen my Zoey in two years. Or maybe I would be full of determination, never stopping until I found the truth about my daughter. Standing on a street near a known hangout of Ashworth's, I stopped a woman on the sidewalk.

"Hi." I handed her a flyer. "I'm looking for my daughter. Her name is Katie. Have you seen her?"

The woman pressed her lips into a thin line and turned her body away, barely glancing at the flyer.

"Can you please look?"

She repeated the dismissive attitude and kept on walking. Was this how people were? Did they care so little about a missing person? She didn't even glance at the flyer.

A man with a dirty T-shirt and equally dirty denim swaggered over, holding on to the front loop of his pants. "What you got there?"

I handed him a flyer with Katie's picture on it. "I'm looking for my daughter. Her name is Katie. Have you seen her around here?"

He studied the photo and said, "Haven't seen a girl like that around here."

"Thank you. Can you hold on to this in case you see her? Maybe ask around?"

"Sure." He accepted the flyer and kept on walking down the street.

This went on for nearly an hour before we spotted Ashworth. Based on our prior surveillance, he came by the same corner store every single day. As he was about to walk into the store, I said, "Excuse me," and handed him the flyer. "I'm looking for my daughter. Have you seen her?"

He looked down at the picture and paused, cocked his head before pushing it back and saying, "No, I didn't see that lady." He continued into the store. I'd seen recognition in his eyes when he saw Katie's picture.

He could do his shopping. I'd be waiting for him when he returned. While he was inside, I continued to hand out flyers and ask people for their help. Half were helpful and looked at the photo; the other half brushed me off as if I was trying to sell them something they didn't want.

Ashworth came out with a brown paper bag.

"Can you look again?"

"Lady, I don't know that girl."

With my hand in my pocket, I pointed my finger in the shape of a gun and said, "Are you sure?"

His eyes grew to the size of saucers.

Using that fear for my benefit, I grabbed him by his collar

and pulled him over to the alley and said, "Are you sure? Look at the picture again."

"I don't want any trouble."

"You're about to get into a whole world of trouble if you don't start talking to me."

"Who are you, lady?"

Adrenaline flowed as I embodied the role of a mother looking for her daughter. "I'm Katie's mom, and I want to know where she is."

"All right, all right, jeez." I let go of his shirt, and he stepped back. "I may have seen a lady like that, but I don't know where she is now."

He was twitchy, and his eyes darted in all directions. I stepped next to him and pressed my finger gun against his side. "Let's go for a walk." He shuffled along as I said, "Hurry up," until we were down the alley far enough where nobody would see us, then I let him go. "Now I want the truth, or this may be your last day on earth."

"Dang. She must get her viciousness from you."

Her viciousness? We had assumed Kate was an innocent. Was it that she wasn't being held against her will but actually hiding from us?

"I don't know who Katie is." He shrugged his head back and said, "That's not Katie."

"What do you mean that's not Katie?"

His face relaxed. "Dang, you don't know?"

"What don't I know?"

"Your daughter, she's not so innocent. And if she didn't tell you where she's at, maybe she didn't want you to find her."

I shut my eyes, trying to control my rage. I lifted the front part of my jacket to reveal the actual firearm I had in my holster. "Look, I know you work for Atlas, and I think he knows where

Katie is. I want to know everything you know about the person in this photo."

"I don't talk to no police."

"It's your lucky day. I'm not the police. Now, tell me what you know."

"I don't have to talk to you."

Hands on hips, I said, "No, you don't, but you know what I could do to you? I know people who are looking for you, Ashworth Dante. Those people are trying to pin five murders on you for distributing drugs that killed five people. Do you want to go to jail for life? Do you want the Brothers to come after you? Do you want Atlas to come after you? Forget them. At this point in time, they're the least of your worries."

He lifted his hands in defeat. "If I talk, they'll kill me."

"You don't talk to me, I'll kill you. Look, I don't care about your drugs. I don't care if you go to jail or not. I care about Katie and where she is."

"Let me see the picture again."

I handed him the piece of paper, and he took it begrudgingly. He tilted his head. "I know you're saying her name is Katie, but that's not the name she's going by."

Had Katie simply run away to start a new life with a new name? "What name is she going by?"

"She calls herself Fern. All those hippies change their names, say they've shaken off their old life. She's just one of them, living up on that hippie commune, growing vegetables and smoking pot all day."

My heart sank. She had been there the whole time. "You said she's vicious. Is she part of the drug business?"

"Heck yeah, she is. She's like Atlas's right hand, in more than one way, if you know what I mean."

I shook my head, trying to make sense of this. Was Katie a

drug trafficker, just like Atlas? "What is her involvement with Sunny D?"

"Look, I don't know exactly her part, but word on the street is she killed a lady because she was going to talk to the police when she found out what they're really doing in that hippie place."

Katie was not only a drug dealer but a killer, too? It was a rumor that had to be corroborated, but it started to make sense. But if she was a drug-running killer, why had she called Daphne? Was it to tell her she was okay and to get us to stop looking for her? Had we pictured this all wrong? I grasped the handle of my weapon. "What do you know about the Brothers?"

"I don't know much. Look, Atlas introduced me like once. I literally don't know anything except they're scary dudes."

"How did you meet Atlas?"

"Friend of a friend had an opportunity for some clean-cut kids trying to get some extra cash. It seemed easy enough. Once a week, I pick up the supply, and then I give it to the corner dealers. That's all I had to do. I don't know where it's coming from and I didn't ask. They'd kill me."

Baffled by the new information about Katie, I said, "You're sure this is Fern, Katie, that you're talking about?"

"Yeah, she's just as scary as the rest of them. She looks innocent, but she's not. Is she really your daughter?"

"Her parents hired me to find her."

With a look of awe, he said, "Dang, they must have spent a lot of money on you. Some people have all the luck."

Did he not have anyone who cared for him? He didn't seem all that hard for a drug-dealing wannabe. Another lost young person, looking to follow anyone who led them. "Thanks for the tip. Stay safe." With that, I turned.

He called out, "They'll kill me. Can't you put me in protection or something?"

I pivoted back. "Are you worried about your safety?"

"You seem to know what they're about."

He had a point. And realized I blew it talking about the Brothers and needed to take him in so he couldn't tell the others we were onto them. "Stay there. I'll make a call." I stepped back a few feet, keeping my eyes on Ash. "Hey, Hirsch."

"That was intense."

"He wouldn't tell me what I wanted to know."

"Did you hold a gun on him?"

"Of course not. So, what can we do about his safety?"

"I'll call the DEA."

After hanging up, I went back to Ashworth. "We'll see what we can do."

"What are you, like some MacGyver lady?"

"Why aren't you in school?"

"I'm in college."

College kid dealing drugs for a dangerous organization? This case was getting stranger and stranger. "Really?"

"Yep. Got a 3.5 last semester."

"Then why are you out selling drugs?"

"Hey, money's money. Food and rent aren't free. I don't have a mom and dad with deep pockets who could spend big bucks to have a scary lady find me."

"All right, hang tight." I glanced around; we didn't appear to have anybody watching us, which was a good thing. My phone rang, and I answered. "Hey."

"We'll bring him in. Take him back to the station in your car so it doesn't look like he's driving off with law enforcement. The DEA will pick him up at the station."

"Okay."

Cell phone in pocket, I told Ashworth, "You're coming with me."

"Where are we going?" he asked defiantly.

After a tight-lipped frown, I said, "You want to be safe, right?"

"Yeah."

"Come with me, and you'll be safe. Deal?"

"Okay."

With a nod of approval, I escorted him to my car, where Vincent waited behind the wheel. I opened up the back door and said, "Get inside."

"Who's that?"

"My partner. Get inside."

He slid in, and I said, "Put your seatbelt on." He gave me a look like he didn't know what to make of me.

Good. He needed to be afraid. Maybe not of me, but of who might come after him. I climbed into the car next to Vincent.

"How did it go?"

"You're not going to believe it." Because I barely could. Had Katie really chosen a life of crime?

36

—————

HIRSCH

With Ash in DEA custody, we got an earful about Atlas and Katie, also known as Fern. We had been surprised by the revelation that Fern, or Katie, wasn't known to the DEA by name but Atlas's girlfriend had been mentioned by a CI. Notably, she had allegedly killed a woman who had wanted to leave the commune in Jenner and turn them in. Our Sunny D death investigation and missing person case were the most peculiar we'd worked yet, but nothing had prepared me for what happened next.

What had once been a vibrant blue SUV was now an unrecognizable pile of mangled metal and shattered glass. The hood of the vehicle had crumpled like paper, and the engine block was destroyed. It seemed impossible that the driver had survived. The asphalt had diamond-like shards of fractured glass shimmering in the morning light.

The car had crashed into a street lamp, knocking it to a strange angle, its stem bent and twisted. A band of yellow police tape was stretched across the perimeter of the area, preventing the onlookers from getting too close to what remained of the accident.

A uniformed officer stood outside the crime scene tape.

"Are you the responding officer?" I asked.

"Yes, sir."

After a flash of my badge and explanation I'd spoken to his superior officer, I said, "What happened here?"

"Witness statements say the car veered off, and a lady scrambled out before it hit. She went back and then ran off."

"Only one vehicle involved?"

"That's right."

Based on the severity of the crash, it had to be intentional or the driver had used excessive speed and lost control. "Where are the witnesses to the accident?"

"It's the older couple next to the gray car. They're the ones who called it in."

"Do we know the whereabouts of the woman who ran from the scene?"

"No. By the time I got here, she was gone."

"Driver status?"

"Surprisingly, he's alive. They rushed him over to County Hospital. Head injury, broken arm and leg."

"Do you have a name on the driver?"

I knew the name because a surveillance team had been following him but were three cars back and didn't see exactly what happened. Unsure of his medical status, they didn't want to lose him and let the woman run off without following her. I wished they would have followed, but I understood their logic. Split-second decisions can be right or wrong, and you have to go with your gut.

"The registration says Jackson Galen."

"Thank you. I'll talk to the witnesses."

"Anytime, Sergeant."

The streets were busy and noises from traffic were loud as I walked over to an elderly couple who stared out at the wreckage. They were holding on to one another. The sheer horror of the scene was palpable. "Hello, my name is Sergeant Hirsch. I was told you witnessed the accident."

The man said, "It happened so fast. It was the strangest thing I had ever seen."

The woman said, "It was terrifying."

"Can you tell me exactly what you saw?"

The man said, "We were driving along, and they were next to us, and they were going really fast, and then it veered off. And seconds later, a woman sprang from the passenger side of the car, rolled onto the ground and the car hit the pole. It was like this awful loud thud. We couldn't believe our eyes. The woman ran back into the car. We thought she must've been checking on the driver, but then a few seconds later, she emerged from the wreckage and ran off."

That was odd. But considering what we had learned, it was consistent. "What direction did she go?"

The man pointed down the street.

"Had you ever seen the woman or the man before?"

"No."

"Do you remember what the woman looked like?"

"The one thing I could tell you was that she was younger with reddish-blonde or blonde hair, maybe a young adult in her 20s or 30s. It was hard to tell. It all happened so fast."

With my cell phone, I retrieved a photo of Katie and handed it to the woman. "Could this have been the girl?"

The woman pulled down her glasses and squinted. "It's hard to tell, but maybe."

Had we found Katie and let her run away? "Did she appear to be injured?"

"She moved like the dickens. She didn't seem to be slowed down by anything."

Was it Katie and she was running for her life? Had she

caused the accident? After what we had learned from Ashworth the day before, I had to wonder. Assuming he wasn't full of it. Was Katie on the run from Atlas and the Brothers or from the police? All three? "Thank you. You've been very helpful."

"I hope that girl's okay," the woman added.

"Me too."

With as many details as I would get, I called Martina. "Hey, I'm in Concord, on the corner of Lemon and Ygnacio. There's been a car accident. The driver, Atlas a.k.a. Jackson Galen a.k.a Ryan Harris, was transferred to County Hospital. A woman was seen running from the car. It could have been Katie."

I must admit, I hadn't seen this coming. Had Katie tried to kill Atlas? How else could she have had the time to think to jump out before the car hit the pole? And why did she return to the car before hurrying off?

"It's likely Katie."

"That's what I'm thinking. I'm about to call the DEA and assign protection on Atlas's hospital room in case the Brothers come after him."

"Okay, I'll be right over with a team to search for Katie."

"Sounds like a plan." Was the woman Katie? It had to be, based on what Ashworth told us. If he wasn't lying to us to save his own rear end. If he was truthful, Atlas was still Katie's boyfriend, which meant she was most likely to be the person with him. But where the heck did she go?

37

———

FERN

Gasping for air, I stumbled in front of a small, dilapidated house with a brown, withered lawn. I had lost all track of time. My only focus was on putting one foot in front of the other. I didn't know where I was, but I knew I needed to get away from the cops and away from Atlas.

For four days, I had meticulously planned my escape from Atlas, but the thought of where I'd go when I was free hadn't crossed my mind. That was pretty shortsighted of me. I should've realized I needed a plan, especially since I'd added another offense to my long list of crimes. Murder, drug trafficking, and I may have killed Atlas.

There was blood everywhere. On the seats, on the dashboard, and dripping from Atlas. I hadn't planned to kill him. The accident was intended to incapacitate him long enough for me to escape. I didn't regret my actions, but when I saw his ashen face as I reached to grab his wallet and cell phone, he looked dead. He wasn't moving, there was blood all over his face, and his leg was in an unnatural position. I'd nearly been sick.

Free from Atlas, I had to consider my next move. If I wasn't afraid of going to jail, I could seek the police for help, but that was risky. Once they learned the truth, how long would they put me in prison for? Probably for the rest of my life.

Maybe I could make a deal. Tell them what I knew about the Brothers and Atlas's involvement. If I did, they might reduce my sentence. I hadn't wanted to kill that woman. I really hadn't, and I was sick about it. As I lay awake at night, I thought about her family and friends who would never know her fate. They must be so confused and wondering where their daughter ran off to. Did my parents and friends ever wonder about me? Somebody had. Otherwise, that private investigator wouldn't be following Atlas and questioning him about me. But who? I wouldn't think it was my parents. Dad was probably glad I was gone. Had it been Daphne?

Since Opal's death, I thought about my family and old friends a lot and came to the conclusion I couldn't go home. Who knows what my dad would do to me? He'd probably take zero pity on me if I asked for their help. The only friend I thought might even talk to me was Daphne. Would she still be my friend if she found out all the things I'd done? I wouldn't blame her if she didn't want to see me or talk to me ever again, but at that point, she was my only hope.

Scanning the neighborhood, I saw there weren't many people out. I hurried toward the mailbox and flipped it open, pulling out a piece of mail and reading the address to the home. Concord. Daphne didn't live far from Concord. After I slid the envelope back inside, I closed the lid to the box and hurried down the street. Behind a row of juniper bushes, I crouched down and dialed Daphne's number. The phone rang in my ear. What if she wasn't home, or she didn't recognize the number and refused the call?

"Hello?" she finally said.

Oh, thank the heavens. "Daphne."

"Katie, is that you?"

Tears streamed down my cheeks upon hearing her voice. I wasn't prepared for how emotional the reunion would be. But she was a symbol of everything I'd left behind. Friendship, being goofy and silly, being free.

"Yes, it's me."

"Where are you?" she asked, with a hint of worry in her voice.

"I'm in Concord. I need your help."

Would she help me? I wasn't sure.

"What do you need?"

Was I asking for too much after everything I had done? "Could you come pick me up?"

"Give me the address."

Hesitating, I wondered if I deserved her friendship or her help. After a deep breath, I gave her the address from the mailbox. If Daphne was willing to help me with no questions asked, maybe all hope wasn't lost.

38

———

MARTINA

After a thorough search of the neighborhood surrounding the crash site, there was no sign of Katie, or Fern, or whoever the woman was that caused the car accident sending Atlas to the hospital. There were only a few "maybes" when I showed her photo to passersby. I was operating under the assumption the woman who fled the scene was, in fact, Katie, based on Hirsch's interviews of the eyewitnesses. Without additional information, it was the most logical conclusion.

Quite the twisted turn of events.

What was I supposed to say to Katie's parents? That she was alive, on the run, and possibly a murderer? What had driven Katie to such a dark path? Was it her abusive father or her desire to be young and free, without having to live up to others' expectations?

My phone buzzed. *My girl.* "Hi, Zoey. What's up?"

"Are you going to be home soon?"

"I'll probably wrap up here pretty soon. Why?"

"Well, you've been working so much lately. I was wondering if you wanted to have an old-fashioned movie night like we used to."

My heart skipped a beat. It had been months since Zoey and I had held our tradition. She'd been so busy with all her extracurricular activities I was thinking she didn't want to hang out with me anymore, and it hurt like a bee sting. She was sixteen, independent, and every minute of her day was filled with something to do: sports, acting, academic decathlon, and, of course, friends. "You don't have any plans tonight?"

"No. Kaylie wanted to hang out, but it's been too long since you and I hung out."

My eyes welled up. Searching for Katie, a young woman who had run away from home so fast she fell into the arms of a criminal, made me even more grateful for my Zoey. "I'll be home soon."

"Can I order pizza?"

Zoey and her pizza. It was astounding she was so thin. "Sure, can you also order a salad?"

"Of course. See you soon. Love you, Mom."

"Love you, too."

She hung up, and I thanked the Lord for such a wonderful daughter. We started butting heads the day she turned thirteen, but she was still the sweet, outgoing Zoey she'd always been. Did she understand how much her wanting to spend time with me meant? I had heard so many horror stories about teenagers, and I figured Zoey would be no different. Heck, I was a nightmare on wheels when I was a teen. It was surprising I ever survived it. I took one last look at the area—nothing but cars whizzing past, no sign of a pedestrian on the run.

Where was Katie? And the more pressing question, what had she become?

It wasn't likely I'd get answers that night. It was time to call it a day and go home to Zoey. I called Hirsch. "The team canvassed a dozen blocks, asking people if they'd seen her. No luck. Only a few said Katie looked vaguely familiar, and it could have been her. Any word on Atlas's condition?"

"He's out of surgery. They think he'll make it, but he's not awake yet. The doctor said he will be heavily medicated for a while, and they're keeping him overnight for observation. There's some concern about brain swelling."

"Is there a possibility he won't make it?"

"They said it's a remote possibility. I have two officers guarding his room in case the Brothers try to take him out."

Was Katie working for the Brothers? Or was she simply trying to escape from Atlas? "If it was Katie who caused the accident, what are you thinking in terms of motive?" I asked.

"That's a good question. She could be armed and dangerous. She could be working on behalf of the Brothers. Maybe they instructed her to take Atlas out."

The way her parents had described her, it seemed unfathomable that Katie was a killer and working for a drug organization. But people were definitely capable of change. Unfortunately, it was not always for the better. "All right, I'll tell the rest of the team to wrap up and head out."

"Are you going back to the sheriff's department?"

"No, I'm heading home. Zoey has a free night and wants to do an old-fashioned movie night."

"I sense pizza and ice cream in your future. How long has it been?"

"Too long. I'm taking every opportunity she gives me to spend time with her."

"I understand."

I knew he did. He had a daughter of his own and knew what it was like to watch them grow up at lightning speed right before your eyes.

When Zoey was an infant, she was the brightest thing in my

life, and she still was. I said, "I'll let you go," as I walked back to my car.

"Wait a second."

I stopped. "What?"

"Isn't tomorrow night your big date?"

How could I forget? "I wouldn't call it a big date, but yes, it's a date." I found myself grinning once again. Dang it. My poker face was the worst.

"If I don't talk to you before your date, I hope you have a good time."

"Thanks, Hirsch. Stay safe." With that, I ended the conversation and thought, *TGIF*. We'd resume our search for Katie and the Brothers another day.

As I proceeded toward my car, the idea I was going to spend the evening with my daughter and my dog brought me joy, and a tiny bit of sadness too. I knew these days were numbered.

39

―――――――

HIRSCH

Audrey squealed as I pushed her on the swing. She kept calling out, "Higher, higher!"

Audrey loved going to the park and playing on the swings. Her love of swings and her desire to go higher and higher made me think she might be a thrill-seeker. At five years old, she was already showing signs of her true personality. A born leader, she invited me to many tea parties with her teddy bears, where she dictated seating arrangements and the proper way to drink tea out of tiny plastic cups. Her interests seemed to revolve mostly around art and animals.

Kim strolled over with a couple of coffees. "I'll never tire of that sound."

She was referring to Audrey's giggles. "I don't think I will either. I was just talking to Martina yesterday. She was telling me she was having a movie night with Zoey. They used to do that every single Friday night when Zoey was younger."

"That sounds like a nice tradition."

"Yeah, but Martina says it pretty much stopped when Zoey became a teenager. She hung out with her friends instead or was too busy with extracurricular activities."

"I suppose that'll be Audrey one day."

When Audrey spotted Kim, she said, "Mommy, Mommy, look at me!"

"Wow, you're so high up there! Aren't you scared?"

Audrey shook her head as I pushed her again, and she squealed. "I guess we have to remember to cherish every single one of these moments."

"Absolutely. Actually, I was kinda thinking..."

I pushed Audrey as she returned and glanced at my gorgeous wife. "What?"

"Well, Audrey's five, and everything is going well with the nanny. What if we had another one?"

We were content with one child, but the thought had crossed my mind—would two be even better than one? "Do you want to start trying, like now?"

Kim's smile widened. "I'm ready."

For my wife and family, I'd do anything. We had a nanny and could figure out how to make it work. "I would love that." Hugging Kim, I missed my opportunity to push Audrey.

"Daddy, push me!"

Admittedly, I was a sucker for anything Audrey wanted. I gave Kim a light kiss on the lips before freeing myself and pushing Audrey again. With my arm around Kim's waistline, I continued to push Audrey with my free hand. I didn't think life could get any better than in that moment.

My phone buzzed, and I pulled away. Checking the screen, I said, "I gotta take this."

She gave a reassuring nod. Kim had gotten used to the phone calls I had to take. She was an understanding woman and a supportive wife. It didn't mean she didn't get frustrated sometimes, but mostly, it hadn't been too disruptive to our lives. "This is Hirsch."

"Agent Bishop here. I have some intel I thought I'd share."

"What is it?" I stepped back, and Kim took over the duty of pushing Audrey on the swing.

"I received some intel the Brothers are back in the Bay Area. One of their enforcers is with them."

"Are they after someone? Do you think they know Atlas is in the hospital? Worried he'll talk?"

"Maybe, or maybe because he's been in the hospital, he hasn't been in contact with them, and they're worried he's on the run or something. Who knows, but these are bad guys."

I tilted my head down and back up again. I needed to let Martina know. But she was on a date; it would have to wait.

"We've also been asking around about Fern, also known as Katie. Passing her photo around. Apparently, she's feared, but she usually just follows Atlas's orders. It's possible she was trying to get away from Atlas, or the other possibility is she could be working for the Brothers. Maybe because she didn't finish Atlas off, they came to do it. The CI didn't seem to know if they wanted to get rid of Atlas, only that they were coming to see him."

"And Fern?" Or Katie or whoever she was.

"If they're looking for Atlas, they're looking for Fern."

"All right, thanks. We'll be on the lookout. We still haven't located Katie, or Fern."

"Let us know if you find anything."

"Will do."

Phone in pocket, I stepped back over to Kim.

"You have to go?"

"No, just the DEA giving us some information on a case."

She raised her brows. "Sounds dangerous." She must have sensed my uneasiness and said, "I know you can handle yourself. I can't help but worry about you. But I know it's your job, and it's who you are. I've noticed how you've been so energetic and bright since working with Martina again. If you want to go back to a more active role in investigations, you won't get a fight from me. I want you to be you, August. That's who I fell in love with."

"What about you, Audrey, and the next one?"

"We can handle it."

Could she? I wasn't sure she fully understood what the life of a homicide detective's family entailed. Missed dinners and soccer games would be commonplace. "I'll think about it."

Later that night, after dinner, I was relaxing with Kim on the couch. My phone alerted me to an incoming call. "This is Hirsch."

"Agent Bishop here. One of our Bay Area CIs told us the Brothers went to the hospital to talk to Atlas."

Why hadn't the officers guarding the room notified me? "So, they're definitely in town for Atlas. Have they gotten to him yet? I have two guards on him."

"They tried. Saw the guards and left. The CI told us they were headed for Fern next. They don't know what went down, but the Brothers are out for blood."

"Sounds like she's in trouble." I'd need to check in with the officers guarding Atlas's room to see if there were any sightings of Katie and put out an APB to keep her safe.

"If she's unarmed and on her own, absolutely. Between you and me, those are a couple of guys I would not want hunting me."

After thanking Agent Bishop, I called over to the guards outside Atlas's room. "This is Hirsch. Everything okay over there?"

"All quiet," the officer said.

I explained the development, and they promised to be on the lookout for anything suspicious. Call ended, I needed to tell Martina. Katie was her missing person. It would be a shame to have nearly located her and then lose her to the Brothers. About to dial, I hesitated. She was on her date with Wilder. I didn't want to ruin it for her; she deserved happiness away from the job. But this was important. Really important.

I began pacing.

"You okay?" Kim asked, watching me with concern.

"I need to talk to Martina, but she's on a date."

Kim gave me a look I knew well. It was one of those, "You don't seriously think she wouldn't want you to call" looks.

"If I know Martina at all, she'd want you to call her." Kim was right. She was always right.

40

———————

MARTINA

My belly hurt from laughing so much. "There's no way that's true," I managed to say between fits of laughter.

"I swear, it totally happened."

Smiling, I realized it had been a long time since I'd had such a fun night with a man, no less a romantic interest, and I had to admit I was interested. He was handsome, charming, smart, and funny.

"You've probably never done anything so stupid in your younger years, not even in college," he said, clearly probing.

"Oh, the number of stupid things I've done... I could fill an entire novel. But, full disclosure, I didn't go to college," I revealed.

"No?"

"Well, I took a series of business classes after I took on the partnership with Stavros, but no. I was in the Army for four years, and then I got married and had Zoey. Zoey was a surprise, so I put my plans for college on hold. But before the Army, stupid was my middle name."

"I'm intrigued," he said, grinning at me. "I'm sure you and your besties got into it."

"Oh, we did. I think I told you I'm a recovering alcoholic?" He nodded respectfully. "Well, I wasn't in recovery back in my teenage years, and my best friend and I got into all the trouble. I grew up on Stone Island, so there wasn't a lot to do other than get up to mischief. One night, the two of us snuck onto one of our neighbors' boats and took it out for a joyride."

"A lawbreaker, huh?" he asked incredulously.

"That was probably the least of my offenses," I said with a smile.

"You and your friend... are you still close?"

With a heaviness in my heart, I said, "The summer after senior year, she disappeared. Thirteen years later, I found her, murdered."

"I'm so sorry. That must've been really rough."

Focusing on gratitude, I had to be thankful we found her and she didn't remain in that lonely grave with her family and loved ones wondering what happened to her. "It was. It was one of those situations where everyone thought she was a runaway and didn't bother looking for her. But I knew in my heart she hadn't run away. She would've told me—we were best friends. Not that she hadn't kept her secrets, but when we found her, it all made sense, and I grieved for her all over again. Actually, it was the first case I worked with Hirsch."

"You're kidding?"

It was funny to think my best friend Donna, in death, had led me to Hirsch, one of the best friends I ever had. "Our cases overlapped, kind of like our current case, and well, the rest is history."

"I'm very sorry for your loss, but in some ways, I'm glad you met Hirsch, started working with the Cold Case Squad, and met Jayda," he said, blushing ever so slightly.

He was cute when he was embarrassed. "I agree. You know,

sometimes bad things happen in the world for no good reason, but sometimes, most of the time, there is a silver lining."

"My wild tales from college—you found them amusing?"

"You didn't think when I nearly spit out my iced tea, it was a sign I was amused?" I responded, grinning at him.

"I wasn't sure if you were laughing with me or at me."

He'd definitely get a second date—if he wanted one. "Definitely with you. But does it bother you I don't drink or that I'm in AA?" I asked him.

"Not at all. I'm actually not a big drinker myself. I like a glass of wine with dinner, but that's about it. And I think it's cool you're a sponsor. It's admirable."

"Yeah, it's new, but I love it. I wanted to give back to those who need my help, since Zoey has been growing up and needing me less."

My smile faded as I spoke, and it made me think about best friends and old times. What if Donna, my best friend from high school, had showed up fifteen years later and called me for help? There was no question I would have helped. Was Katie Daphne's Donna? How dense of me to not have realized it sooner.

"Did I lose you?" he asked.

"I'm so sorry. No, the talk about best friends in high school and college made me think of the case I'm working on. It's a missing person we think is on the run, but I just realized I might know where she is."

"So, I'm also helping with your case? I feel like there is no downside to us seeing each other," he said with a smirk.

Our eyes met, and I said, "I see zero downside." I felt tingly all the way down to my toes. It had been so long since I'd felt the sensation, I'd forgotten what it was like.

My phone buzzed, and he said, "Do you need to take that?"

"I should, and I'm so sorry."

He tilted his head and raised his brows. "Take it. You're a mother and someone who saves lives for a living."

"You won't be upset?"

With a reassuring wink, he said, "Do it. Answer it, or I'll be offended."

Seeing the caller ID, I lifted my finger and stepped away from the table. "What's up? I'm out with Wilder."

"I'm so sorry to interrupt your date." Hirsch paused. "It's getting late. It must be going well."

"Is that why you're calling?"

"No."

Part of me was glad he'd called. I wanted to tell him my thoughts about Katie's location. "What is it, Hirsch?"

"The DEA called. The Brothers are in the Bay Area, and they have good information they're going after Katie or Fern, assuming Fern is Katie."

"I think I know where she is."

"You do?"

"I should've thought of it earlier. Who would she run to if not her parents? Her best friend, who she's already reached out to once. I need to get ahold of Daphne."

"I can call over to Daphne's. You finish your date."

Glancing back at Wilder, I assumed he had read my expression because he dropped his chin and gave me a look that said he knew I needed to leave. "No, I'll call over to Daphne's. She knows me."

"All right, let me know if you need backup."

"Thanks, Hirsch." I hurried back to Wilder. "We think my missing person is in danger, and I have a feeling I know where she is and..."

"And you need to go?" He said it with a playful expression.

"Would you hate me if I leave now?" I asked him, feeling both nervous and guilty.

"I won't hate you on one condition," he said, standing up.

"And what's that?"

"You promise me a second date when your case is over; when your missing person is safe."

"It's a deal," I said, feeling grateful to have met such an understanding person. We had finished dinner and were just waiting for dessert, but still. "I should really go now."

"Be the best Martina there is," he said encouragingly.

He leaned in and butterflies swam around in my belly. I did the same and our lips brushed. A shot of electricity arced through me. After a moment, I leaned back and said, "Dinner soon."

"Go," he said, giving me an encouraging nod.

The date and my first kiss since Jared died had me reeling. Not to mention the realization I may find Katie—if I could get to her in time.

As soon as I was outside, I dialed Daphne's number. It rang and rang and went to voicemail. That was a bad sign, or she wasn't home. Either way, I wasn't taking any chances.

I called Hirsch back. "Daphne isn't answering her phone. I'm heading over to her apartment. Can you order me backup? A couple of patrol cars outside would be good. It'll take me twenty minutes to get there."

"I'll call it in, and I'll meet you there," he assured me.

I hung up, butterflies swirling and adrenaline rushing. I hadn't felt this high since, well, since I was high. And in that moment, I thought maybe I could have it all: a romantic partner, a daughter, and a crazy, exciting job. As I rushed over to Daphne's, I said a silent prayer, hoping that we would find Daphne and Katie safe and sound.

41

FERN

Being with Daphne, I felt safe and got glimpses of who I used to be. Daphne was still young at heart, untarnished, and had just graduated from college. I envied her and how simple and safe her life was. After a tearful reunion, she sat me down and gave me a glass of water and something to eat before offering me her home. After the best shower of my life, she lent me some clean clothes and her bed.

Refreshed from a good night's sleep and a relaxing day, I met Daphne at her dining table. She was sipping on hot tea. She offered me a cup, but I politely declined and grabbed a tall glass of water. It was time to come clean, body and spirit.

Face-to-face, I sat across from her. "I'm guessing you have questions." She'd been gracious enough to let me explain at my own pace. I wasn't sure I had her same patience.

"Where have you been?" Daphne asked.

"I was with Atlas."

"Your parents said they went to Chico, but nobody had ever heard of Atlas. That's not where he lived. Where have you been, Katie?"

I crinkled the napkin in front of me; the sound echoed in the otherwise quiet room. I was unsure exactly how much to tell her. I needed her, and I didn't want her to reject me after she knew the awful truth. But if I held back, I was being Fern, and I didn't want to be Fern anymore. My heart ached for the life I had before everything went so very wrong.

"You're right, and I thought we were going to a farm in Chico. I had never been there before. He'd only described it, but then, when we arrived at the farm, it wasn't in Chico. It was up the coast in Jenner. Do you know where that is?" I asked her.

Daphne stared at me in disbelief. "No."

"It's an hour north of Bodega Bay. It's beautiful there. Miles and miles of coastline, tall trees, and endless hiking trails. Breathtaking."

Daphne looked at me with a furrowed brow. "Why didn't you answer any of my calls? If you were in this great place, I don't understand why you wouldn't call."

I knew I had to tell her the truth. It was all going to catch up to me anyhow. She'd been my best friend. I owed her the truth. Did she need every single detail? "Things weren't exactly how Atlas told me they would be. I thought it was going to be him and me, living together as a couple, and there were some of his friends who lived there too. That's what I thought it was going to be like, sort of like a commune."

"Like a cult?" Daphne asked.

Sweat trickled down my back. "No, not a cult. It wasn't like that at first. The first couple of months, we planted vegetables and harvested, and we all cooked together. Atlas and I had this electric connection. Our love deepened, and I thought I was the luckiest person in the world."

"I still don't understand why you never called. I called you almost every day the first month, but you didn't return a single one."

Daphne's pain-filled eyes stared back at me, and I was

ashamed to have caused that. "When I arrived in Jenner, Atlas said they don't use any electricity, cell phones, or landlines. It was an off-the-grid kind of place. We lived off Mother Nature."

"But couldn't you make one last call to say you were fine and where you were?" Daphne asked, the hurt still clear in her voice.

"He told me everyone who lived there had to forsake their old life. A life filled with commercialism, capitalism, and the rotten world full of violence and greed. So, I agreed to give him my cell phone, and we all had to choose new names."

"Let me get this straight," Daphne began, looking puzzled. "Atlas told you that you had to get rid of your phone, you couldn't contact anybody from your old life, and you had to change your name?"

Hearing the words from her mouth, and seeing her obvious suspicion, made it painfully clear how stupid I'd been from the very beginning. It wasn't over time like I had imagined. He suckered me in the second we met. Why hadn't I seen the red flags? No contact with the outside world, a new name. In that moment, I realized that was the exact time he took full ownership of me.

"Hearing it now, yeah, it sounds pretty stupid."

"Didn't you think it was strange he wanted you to give up your whole life and never talk to anybody again?"

Obviously, Daphne was the smarter of us. "At the time, it seemed a little strange, but I trusted him. He brought me to this beautiful place, and it all seemed to fit, like a utopia."

"Okay, so you've been at this utopia for two years, living off the land... so you're happy?"

"That's how it started. I soon learned there was more to it."

Before I could continue to explain why I hadn't contacted her and why I was covered in road rash and bruises, there was a banging on the door. My pulse quickened. "Are you expecting someone?"

Daphne's face paled. "No. Are you?"

Fear filled my being. "No. Don't answer the door. See who it is first."

Daphne hurried to the front door of her apartment and inched her eye up to the peephole. Without warning, she jumped back. "There are some men. They look scary."

My heart was beating so fast. Was it the Brothers? Was it Atlas? I was sure if Atlas was alive, he must be in the hospital. They banged again, and Daphne stepped farther away.

"Open up, Fern. We know you're in there."

They were after me. "That's me. That's... that's the name he had me take."

"Who are those people?"

"I'm not totally sure, but I think they're dangerous." I couldn't put Daphne in danger. I was done putting other people in danger. In order to do that, I had to stop being so selfish. "Get back in the dining room. I'll leave with them, so they don't get to you."

Daphne's eyes were wide. "No, don't go with them. I'll call the police."

They pounded again, and I called out, "I'm coming."

Daphne clutched my arm. "I don't think you should open the door, Katie."

With an enormous, loud bang, the door flung open, revealing three members of the Brothers. Daphne and I clutched one another. "What are you doing here?"

They moved in quickly, closing the door behind them. "Where's Atlas? What did you do to him?"

"Atlas... I don't know... there was a car accident."

"We have questions for you..."

Daphne moved away, clearly afraid of the three men, as she should be.

"Hey, where are you going?" the one with all the tattoos yelled at Daphne. She froze as he pulled out a gun, pointed it at her, and then at me. "Nobody goes anywhere. Sit down."

The head and his second in command whispered, and then tattoos said, "Stand up. We'll go to the bedroom."

Fear filled me. I couldn't let them take us. But I was frozen in place. He pressed the nozzle of the gun to my forehead and said, "Now."

Shaking, I barely had the strength to stand up and walk toward the bedroom. Daphne, with tears pouring out of her eyes, followed. Inside the bedroom, the man with the gun said, "Sit down."

"What do you want?" I asked.

"We're missing a few things. We think you know where they are."

"How did you find me?"

"You've got Atlas's phone, don't you?"

With as much confidence as I could muster, I said, "Yes."

"Yeah, well, that's a Brothers phone. There's a tracker, idiot."

A phone tracker? Was there an end to my stupidity? "I don't know anything."

He pulled back the safety and pressed the gun to my forehead once again. "Don't lie to me."

Daphne sat next to me sobbing uncontrollably, and I regretted putting her in danger. It was one thing for them to kill me, but Daphne was innocent. She'd never done anybody any harm. She was my only true friend, and I might get her killed. My worst crime yet.

42

———

MARTINA

THE PARKING LOT at Daphne's apartment was unremarkable, with no indication of anything out of the ordinary. Our police backup hadn't arrived, and from a quick scan of the parked cars, neither had Hirsch. Admittedly, I may have gone over the speed limit a tad.

With a mounting sense of worry, I tried not to think about Wilder because I had to stay focused on Daphne and Katie. The smart thing to do was wait for backup. Too full of adrenaline, sitting and waiting was not an option. Parked, I called Daphne's phone again but was met with the sound of her ringtone followed by her voicemail message. If I'd known what kind of car Daphne drove, I could see if it was in the parking lot. Easily remedied. There was one person I knew who could help and had told me she would, day or night. I dialed Rosemary from the sheriff's department. "Hey, Rosemary, it's Martina."

"What's up?"

"I need you to look up a make, model, and license plate number for me. Daphne Lanter."

"Okay. Give me a sec."

In the old days, I would have called Vincent, but he was off today, and the police had quicker access than Drakos Monroe. Dang. I realized I should have called Vincent since I was working the case with him. Hirsch and I had fallen back into our old pattern so quickly, Vincent hadn't crossed my mind. Not that he'd be upset, but I owed him a text in the morning or when I found Katie.

"Okay, I have it. Silver Toyota Corolla, California license plate number..."

With the phone to my ear, I climbed out of the car, and said, "Thanks, Rosemary," and hung up as I scanned the parking lot, looking for Daphne's car.

After a minute, I found it parked in a carport. She should be home, unless she was out and a friend had picked her up. She was a young woman; if she was on a date or had company, it could explain why she wasn't answering her phone.

Well, if that was true, I would apologize profusely for bothering her, but everything in my being was telling me I needed to check on her. A check of the parking lot confirmed backup still hadn't arrived. It wouldn't hurt to just check outside her apartment and see if anything was amiss. I could peek in through the window and ensure she was okay.

Convinced it was the best plan of action, I hurried toward her first-floor apartment, trying to walk quietly, to not disturb or alert anyone to my presence. When I reached her door, I gasped and stepped back.

It was slightly ajar.

That was never a good sign.

I hurried around the corner and texted Hirsch.

At Daphne's. Door ajar. Looks like someone has kicked it in.

Somebody had broken into Daphne's apartment and Daphne's car was in the parking lot.

She was in serious trouble.

My phone alerted, and I answered the call from Hirsch. "Martina, don't go in without backup."

From the direction of Daphne's apartment, I heard a slight whimper. "Hirsch, I can't wait. I just heard something. Somebody's broken in. She's in danger. I can't just stand by and let this happen."

"I'm about two minutes out. Can you wait two minutes?"

"Would you wait two minutes?" After a pause, I said, "I'll see you when you get here," and placed the phone back into my pocket. Thankfully, the dress I had purchased for my date had pockets. It had been so long since I had bought a new dress, I didn't know the feature existed. I couldn't believe I was wearing a dress, and I was about to enter a very dangerous situation with only a prayer and my combat training.

Strong body, strong mind.

Ready for anything, I crept toward the door and surveyed it once more. Scuff marks, splintered edges—it looked like they had tried to close it behind them, but it no longer set correctly. I slowly pushed the door open and glanced around. The living room was empty. The kitchen, to the right, was clear too. I could hear men's voices; they were in the bedroom.

Quietly, I tiptoed into the kitchen and spotted a block of knives. Thank goodness Daphne loved to cook. As quietly as I could, I pulled the chef's knife from the block, hid it behind my back, and called out, "Daphne, are you home?"

There were hushed whispers—not a very covert operation. "I'm in here," she said, her voice shaking, obviously terrified. I stepped toward the bedroom and spotted the men; one had a gun aimed right at my face.

"Who are you?"

"I'm friends with Daphne. We had plans tonight."

He turned to look at Daphne, who nodded nervously. "Get on the bed," he ordered.

Keeping the knife hidden behind me, I did as he said. The woman sitting next to Daphne stared at me, and I gave her a quick head nod. She didn't know who I was, but I had no doubt in my mind that I was staring at Katie Kimble. My instincts were correct—Katie was "Fern," and these were the Brothers who'd been looking for her.

"What's going on?" I asked, forcing my voice to shake, to blend in. They didn't need to know I was armed and combat-ready.

"You two, shut up. We're here for Fern."

Nice manners. "Do you want me to go?"

The man with sandy blond hair and dark blue eyes turned to look at me and said, "Are you dumb? Sit there and be quiet unless you would prefer to die."

He tried to be scary—and he kinda was—but he wasn't holding a weapon. All he had was his size. If I could catch him by surprise, I'd have a chance against him. Fidgeting on the bed, I kept my eyes on Katie and Daphne until one man, with dark hair, started pacing. "Do I know you?" he asked.

"I don't... I don't know how you would know me," I replied innocently.

"How do you and Daphne know each other?" he asked.

I recognized him from the surveillance photos; he was the head of the operation. "I'm friends with her mom." It was the best I could think of.

"It's awfully late. What were your plans tonight?"

"We were going to a cooking class."

"At 10 o'clock at night?"

"She didn't show up, so I was concerned. That's why I'm here. Obviously, I had a reason to be concerned."

The blond-haired dummy said, "I don't like you."

I thought, *Well, that's something you and I have in common. I don't like you much either.* The tattooed man with the gun, who I also recognized from the surveillance photos, interrupted my thoughts. He barked, "You shut up. Don't make a move or a bullet's gonna find its way to your brain." He then pointed his weapon at Katie and said to her, "One last time. Where are the bars?"

Was he referring to the bars of soap we suspected they were filling with drugs?

"I swear, I don't know," Katie whimpered.

The man's threat grew colder. "You talk by the count of three, or I'll put a bullet in your friend." He turned the gun toward a near-hysterical Daphne.

This situation was escalating far too quickly. I knew I had to do something. There were three of them and three of us. Granted, the other two with me were not trained in combat, but if they were smart enough, they could run.

The man, whom we'd identified as Rafael Peña, counted. "Three. Two..."

Now or never. I lunged at Peña, tackling him to the carpet and kneeing him in the groin. He recovered quickly and placed his hands on my throat as I straddled him. I slashed at his hands before planting my knee on his throat.

The other two men were too stunned to move as I screamed for Katie to grab the gun. But soon enough, the other two men charged at me.

Threatening, I yelled, "Back off or I'll cut your carotid." They were too quick and knocked me off Peña. One pinned my arms while the other sat on my legs.

The man clutching my arms said, "And now, you're going to die."

With too many thoughts bubbling in my mind, I prayed it wouldn't end like this.

43

———

MARTINA

Sweat trickled down my face as I prayed backup would arrive. It all happened so fast, and I couldn't help but question myself. Why had I thought I could overpower three men? I'd hoped Katie would've picked up the gun, suspecting she had handled one before. But it only took one mistake to ruin the plan.

Then, like music to my ears, Katie shouted, "Don't take a single step closer, or I will shoot!"

An instant later, a loud thud echoed, followed by Daphne's scream. Katie turned and said, "Let her go now, or you'll end up like him." I turned my head to look at the ground, and there was Peña, motionless, a pool of blood forming beneath him. Had it been a fatal shot? The men slowly got up. One said, "Just... just calm down, Fern."

She screamed, "My name is Katie!"

Stunned by the change of events, I didn't move.

"Get up, whoever you are," Katie said.

I stood up slowly, retrieving the knife that had fallen near the edge of the bed. "I'm a friend," I said as I retrieved it.

She eyed me briefly. "Who are you? Are you really friends with Daphne's mom?"

"No, my name is..." I stopped, realizing I didn't need these people to know my name. "I'm an investigator. Your parents hired me to find you, Katie. I've met with Daphne before. I suspected you might be here."

"Are you the police?" she asked.

"No, I'm not."

Daphne blurted out, "It's true. We've met. She was asking about you. She was trying to find you. What she's saying is true, I swear it."

Katie's face fell, and her body went slack. She looked like she was going to break down. I shoved the knife back under the bed and crept up. "Why don't you hand me the gun? It'll be okay. I'm trained in handling weapons." With the gun still pointed at the men, I took it from Katie's shaking hands. She turned toward the exit. "Where are you going?" I asked.

"The police will be here. They'll come after me."

"The police are already on their way, Katie." The men's eyes bulged. "That's right. I'm not the police, but I work with them, and they're on their way."

When sirens sounded, I'd swear God had answered my prayers. "Everybody stay where you are. Katie, get back on the bed."

She didn't fight and made her way over to Daphne, who looked so confused by what was going on. Katie just kept mumbling, "I'm so sorry. I'm so sorry."

"What happened? Why are they here? What are they looking for?" Daphne asked.

"I've got the same question. What are you looking for?" I echoed.

"None of your business," the man with dark-blue eyes snapped.

I wanted to yell that I knew exactly who they were and likely what they were looking for, but they didn't need to know I knew about their drug business. Like a stampede of elephants, boots rushed into the room, and an officer I'd never met before said, "Drop the weapon." I knelt down and set the firearm in front of me.

A team of officers rushed in, grabbed the weapon, and cuffed me along with the others. It was a blur of navy-blue uniforms, officers dragging people in and out. In the sea of faces, there was one noticeably absent that I'd hoped would be among them.

44

HIRSCH

With my foot on the gas, I zoomed into the parking lot but slammed on the brakes as a sound resembling a gunshot reverberated through the air. My heart pounded in my chest as I surveyed the surroundings. Black and white police cars had just pulled up, their lights piercing the night. Hopefully, they'd already called for backup. If not, it was my immediate responsibility. It was always better to be safe than sorry.

After contacting dispatch, I parked my car and trailed behind the stream of officers. As we approached the downstairs apartment, the wail of sirens echoed in the distance. Backup would arrive shortly. We had no clue what we were walking into, other than a situation involving Martina.

An officer stationed at the entrance to Daphne's apartment said, "Can I help you?"

I pulled out my badge, presenting it for his inspection. "Sergeant Hirsch, CoCo County Sheriff's Department. My partner, Martina, is working with the sheriff's department. She's inside."

"Description?"

"A woman, about 5'7", shoulder-length dark brown hair, fair complexion."

Acknowledging my information, he pulled out his radio and announced my arrival to whoever was on the other end. "Go ahead, Sergeant." And he granted me entrance.

After a quick thanks, I hurried past, my heart nearly beating out of my chest. Martina and I hadn't worked together in five years. The thought of losing her when we finally got to collaborate again was unbearable.

Relief washed over me when I spotted Martina sitting, handcuffed, at a dining table with an officer standing nearby. Next to her were two other women, both handcuffed. One of them, I immediately recognized as Katie Kimble.

"I'm Sergeant Hirsch," I introduced myself to the room. "What's going on here?"

"Male gunshot victim in the bedroom. Not sure if he's going to make it. Two other males cuffed in the bedroom with two officers standing watch," one of them replied.

A sense of relief filled me, knowing the women were safe. "Martina is with us," I clarified.

She gave a sheepish grin in response.

"That's what she's been telling me."

"It's true. She used to work for the CoCo County Sheriff's Department back when we had the Cold Case Squad."

The officer squinted his eyes toward Martina. "I thought she looked familiar," he said, addressing Martina.

"Would you let me out of these cuffs? I need to talk to Hirsch."

I gave a nod of approval, and the officer removed Martina's handcuffs.

She rubbed her wrists as if the cuffs had caused her discomfort, though I suspected she hadn't been cuffed for long. Perhaps it was more of a mental strain.

"And the others?" I turned to Martina, awaiting her input.

"Leave them for now. We'll be back," she said before

ushering me into the living room, away from the officers and those currently handcuffed.

Her hair was disheveled, and she had blood splatter on her neck, face, and arms. "It's good to see you," she said, with relief in her voice.

"You too. Nice dress."

"It has pockets."

"Are you okay?"

"I'm fine. It was a little dicey for a bit."

"What happened?" I asked, eager for details.

As she explained the harrowing ordeal she'd just endured, her bravery and recklessness astounded me. "You lunged at a man with a gun, and you weren't even armed?"

"I had a knife, but in hindsight, it wasn't the smartest move. I assumed Katie would get the gun and do exactly what she did, and I was right."

A wry smile crossed my face. *Martina being Martina.* "Thankfully, it worked out this time."

She shrugged. "Yep."

My guess was she regretted her actions, at least a little. "Any idea why they were looking for Katie?" I asked, trying to make sense of the situation.

"They kept asking where their bars were. I think we should check the vehicle that Atlas was driving. Maybe he took some of their drugs, and his partners didn't like it, and that's why they're coming after the two of them," Martina suggested.

"Or he had the drugs, was in the accident, and didn't deliver on time. Maybe he was planning to, but they assumed he'd stolen them."

"But if they went to the hospital and learned he was in an accident, they had to know he didn't steal anything. So, why would they come after Katie?"

"Maybe they're impatient?"

"Perhaps."

Bowled over by the fact Martina had almost been killed, I listened as she discussed it so casually, as if it was no big deal. "Did you say anything about their organization?"

"Nope, I didn't mention it at all. Not to them, not to Katie. I played dumb the whole time."

As frustrated as I was Martina had put herself in danger, she was right; I would've done the exact same thing. But I likely would've been armed and not wearing a flowy dress. "You came straight from your date?"

"I knew I had to get here, Hirsch. Even though I didn't have my gun, and I was wearing this get-up."

She glanced down at her dress, now marred with a rip and what looked like some sort of splatter—probably blood. "Who do we have in there?"

"Based on surveillance photos, Rafael Peña—he's the one who was shot. He's lost a lot of blood and may be down for the count. The other two, I'm guessing, are Kenneth Martin and Jacob Briggs."

"You're kidding?"

"No joke."

No kidding. "I need to call the DEA."

"Agreed. How should we tackle this?"

"I'll call the DEA and get instructions from them. They're in the middle of an operation, and I don't want to ruin it. Although, from what you told me about how this went down, I'm guessing we could charge them for unlawful detainment and attempted murder."

"True. I'll talk to Daphne and Katie. Afterward, we'll reconvene and see what to do with them."

"Good, and I'm glad you're okay."

She patted me on the shoulder. "Me too, partner."

"Hey, before you go. How was the date?"

Despite everything she'd just gone through, a smile spread across her face.

"Really?" I said.

"We'll talk about that later, but yes, I like him."

"Talk about a crazy night."

"You're telling me."

As Martina headed back toward Daphne and Katie, I returned to the officer guarding the door. "I called for additional backup when I pulled up and heard the gunshot."

"I heard it on the radio. Is everything going okay back there?"

"I'm about to go into the bedroom where the suspects are being held. Apparently, that's where the gunshot victim is."

"I called for a bus; they should be here any second."

"Great, thanks," I replied and made my way back through the dining room and into the bedroom. A fellow officer was there, guarding the scene.

"What've you got?" I asked.

"Paramedics should be here soon, but the guy on the floor will not make it. He's DOA," he stated matter-of-factly.

My gaze fell to the lifeless body on the floor. I recognized his tattoos. Martina was right; it was Rafael Peña, the Brothers' enforcer and most deadly partner.

Kenneth Martin sat on the bed, and Jacob Briggs was cuffed and sitting in a chair in the far corner of the bedroom. "Is anybody willing to tell me what went on here?" I asked, trying to glean some information from them.

"We're not talking," Jacob Briggs retorted defiantly.

Kenneth Martin added, "We want our lawyer."

I looked back at Rafael Peña's lifeless body and back at them. "A lawyer didn't seem to help him," I pointed out, showing the stark reality of their situation.

They shook their heads in defiance, choosing to remain

silent. They knew better than to talk to me or anybody else in the room without legal counsel. The officer asked, "Sergeant Hirsch, how do you want to proceed?"

"Keep them here. I'll let you know what to do in a few minutes. I'm going to talk to the ladies to find out what happened."

"Yes, sir," the officer acknowledged.

One last look at the stone-faced Jacob Briggs told me he thought their expensive lawyers would set them free. Well, if they thought that, they were in for a rude awakening.

45

———————

MARTINA

Boy, was I relieved to see Hirsch. I was acutely aware of how the situation could have gone the other way, and I was sure Hirsch knew it, too. It had been a long, long time since I'd found myself in such a prickly situation, and I hadn't liked it one bit. I had relied solely on instinct, trusting that Katie would do the right thing. But I could've been wrong. Katie could've been working with them, and I might have been the one lying in a pool of blood.

In hindsight, I should have gone home. I should have changed my clothes, put my jacket on, and armed myself with something more substantial than a makeshift weapon from the kitchen. That would've been the smart thing to do. However, I had a feeling if I had taken the time to go home first, I might have entered a very different scene. There could be two dead women instead of one drug trafficker who had done Lord knows what.

In the bathroom, I gave myself a once-over in the mirror and realized I was in awful shape. My dress was ripped, and what looked like blood splatter decorated my chest, neck, and arms. With toilet paper and a few drips of water from the faucet, I wiped the carnage from my body, hoping to look less Nightmare on Elm Street and more like Main Street U.S.A.

It was going to be a long night.

In the dining room, Daphne and Katie sat while the officer watched over them like a guard. "I'd like to speak with Daphne in the other room. She's not a suspect in any of this." I glanced over at Katie, and she looked at me as if she were wondering if I knew the truth about her. "Please remove her handcuffs."

Hirsch stepped in at that moment, and the officer looked at him for direction. "Remove the handcuffs from Daphne," Hirsch ordered.

His actions validated my request. I gave the officer a look as if to say, "I told you so." And just like that, Daphne turned to expose her handcuffs, and the officer removed them.

"Daphne, why don't you come with me to the living room, and we can have a conversation?"

She wiped the tears from her eyes and stood up.

Tonight was a night that was likely to stay with Daphne for a long time. Her life was threatened, and they had held her against her will. Plus, she had witnessed a man's death. That's not something you can easily forget.

As Daphne approached me, I asked, "Do you need anything. A glass of water perhaps?"

She looked at me with haunted eyes. "No."

"Okay, come with me. It's going to be okay." We reached the living room, she settled onto the couch, and I took the armchair next to it. "What happened, Daphne?"

"They just burst in," she began.

I stopped her. "I mean, before that. How did Katie get here?"

"Well, yesterday, out of the blue, she called me and said she needed my help. She gave me an address to pick her up. She asked me not to tell anyone."

"Where's this address?" I asked.

"It was in Concord. I can give it to you," she responded.

"Was she staying at that address in Concord?"

"No, she had run from her boyfriend."

It was Katie who ran from the traffic accident. "And then what happened?"

"She asked for my help, for me to pick her up. So, I did. I brought her back here. She was pretty banged up and didn't seem to want to talk. She just kept saying, 'thank you, thank you.' I let her take a shower, lent her some of my clothes, and fed her. She went to bed. I didn't want to push her too hard. She seemed exhausted."

"And what were you doing today? Was she here all day?" I asked Daphne.

"Yes. I didn't know how to act around her. She told me she needed time to think. I wasn't sure what she was going to do next. It took all day for her to open up about where she'd been. But then, in the middle of us talking, we heard this loud banging on the door, and they were yelling for somebody named Fern. They kicked the door in, and one of them had a gun. They brought us into the bedroom, asking Katie where their stuff was. She said she didn't know."

Placing my hand on her shoulder, I reassured her, "You're doing great, Daphne."

"And then you came in. You saw what happened after that. Is that man dead?" she asked, her voice trembling.

"I'm not sure, but most likely," I replied, trying to sound calm and reassuring.

"What has Katie gotten mixed up in?" she asked, her eyes wide with fear.

I couldn't blow our cover, not without the DEA letting us know it was okay to talk about the drugs. "We're trying to learn what happened and what Katie is involved in," I told her vaguely.

"Okay." Daphne was shaking.

"Is there somebody you can stay with?" I asked her.

"I could stay with my parents."

"Why don't you call them and let them know you're coming over? I'll drive you. You're safe now. Those guys in there, they're going to jail. They will not stay out of law enforcement's sight, okay?"

"Okay." She looked around the room.

"Do you need your phone?"

"Yeah, I think it's in the kitchen or in my bedroom."

"I'll find it for you." As I got up to leave, she grabbed my hand.

Clearly, Daphne didn't want to be alone. *Understandable.* "Do you want to go back to the dining room with Katie?"

"Please. I don't want to be alone."

"What you've been through is horrific. You may need to have someone to talk to. Do you have a regular therapist?"

"No."

"I'll recommend someone for you. What happened tonight should never have happened. I'm so sorry."

"Do you do this a lot? Save people, I mean. Like, jump in front of danger?"

I wasn't sure I'd saved anyone. "Not so much anymore."

"You seem so cool and in control."

"This is my job. C'mon, let's go in the other room, and you can call your parents."

We headed back into the dining room, and she sat in the chair next to Katie. I walked into the kitchen and saw her phone plugged into the charger on the wall. I retrieved it and set it down in front of Daphne.

"Thank you," she murmured.

Sitting across from Katie, I said, "We need to talk about what happened." Her lips curled downward, and I worried she would start to cry. I said, "Do you know what the men were looking for?"

In a whisper, she said, "No."

"You said you had to leave so the police wouldn't take you away. Why did you say that?" I had a feeling I knew the answer, but I couldn't let on.

Katie looked away, seemingly ashamed. She stared back at me and said, "I've done some bad things. I don't know why I keep running. The right thing to do would be to turn myself in. I guess it was my survival instinct finally kicking in."

"Whatever you've been mixed up in, we can protect you," I assured her.

Katie stared straight ahead.

"Is there anything you want to tell me?" I asked.

She shook her head.

Katie seemed broken. Had Atlas done that to her? Or was Atlas simply a continuation of what her father started? I said, "What you did back there was brave. You saved my life. I appreciate that. And I'm sure my daughter does too."

"You wouldn't have been here if it wasn't for me," she replied.

She had a point. "Yes, but you didn't have to do that."

"It was the least I could do."

Something was eating away at Katie, but she clearly wasn't ready to talk. "I'm going to talk to Sergeant Hirsch and see what he wants to do next. I'll be back." To Daphne, I said, "Did you speak to your parents?"

"Yes, they're expecting me. But what about Katie?"

"Katie needs to stay with us. As soon as I confer with Sergeant Hirsch, I can take you over to your parents', okay?"

"Okay."

I lifted myself out of the chair, weary from a long day, and made my way to Hirsch. It was going to be a long night. Shootings, unlawful detainment; there would be statement after statement. Hirsch was in the corner, texting on his phone. "Hey. I talked to Daphne. She's going to stay with her parents tonight. Katie isn't talking, but I told her whatever she's into, we could help her, protect her."

"Well, we can protect her from those guys, at least for tonight. I talked to the DEA. They're still deciding the best plan of action. Based on tonight's events, these guys could be put away for multiple charges having nothing to do with Sunny D. The DEA wants us to take them to the sheriff's station, put them under arrest for tonight's charges. The DEA will come down tomorrow and decide what to do."

"We'll take Katie in too?"

"Absolutely. She shot a man."

"In self-defense. In my defense. She saved my life."

"And I am grateful for that," Hirsch said.

"I need to drive Daphne home. Are you going to take Katie in?"

"I'll have patrol take her. But I'll meet you down at the station after you drop off Daphne."

"Like old times."

"Like old times," he echoed.

As I turned, a familiar face beamed back at me. She removed her sparkly red frames and smiled. "Well, well, well. This is a surprise."

We approached Dr. Scribner, and she said, "Wish it was under better circumstances. I can only imagine what the two of you are up to. Sorry I missed the barbecue last weekend. Suppose if I hadn't, I would be caught up."

"We'll have to catch up soon."

"I will hold you to that, Martina. You too, Hirsch. Now that you're the brass, we've missed you too."

"I've missed being there," he replied.

And I believed him.

"Paramedics said I've got a body I should get to. You two take care."

"You too." This was definitely one of the strangest reunions.

"Meet you back at the station, Hirsch." After I dropped off Daphne, I wanted to call Vincent to let him know we found Katie. But it was awfully late, and I thought better of it. There was no reason to wake him up at this hour.

46

———

MARTINA

After a few hours of sleep, I returned to the sheriff's station to question Katie. As of the wee hours of the morning, she still wasn't talking, but I hoped she'd have a change of heart after spending some time in a holding cell. The DEA was on their way to decide what to do with the criminals we arrested the previous night. Vincent, Hirsch, and I entered the conference room to meet Katie.

"Morning, Katie. I want to introduce you to my partner, Vincent Teller. He and I were hired by your parents to find you."

"Hi," she said, guarded.

"And I'm guessing you remember Sergeant Hirsch from last night?"

Katie didn't say a word. Maybe she wasn't willing to talk to law enforcement. "We'd like to know what happened, Katie, starting with two years ago when you disappeared from your family and friend's lives."

Katie squinted her eyes. "That's all you want to know about?"

Perhaps Katie was more intuitive than I gave her credit for. "We'd like to start there."

She glanced over at Hirsch and said, "Does he have to be here?"

Hirsch replied, "Not if it makes you uncomfortable."

Katie fidgeted and said, "I prefer not to talk to the cops."

I gave Hirsch a look, and he exited the conference room. Obviously, we would tell him everything Katie told us, but it couldn't be used against her in a court of law. "Are you willing to tell us what happened?"

"My mom and my dad are looking for me?"

She seemed surprised.

"Yes, they both came to my office and talked to Vincent and me. They're worried about you."

Her eyes widened. "Even my dad?" she repeated in shock.

"Your mother led most of the conversation."

With a slight head shake, she said, "I'm surprised they agreed to pay anything to find me."

"Your mother loves you very much," I assured her.

Katie remained silent.

I pressed on. "Where did you go two years ago, Katie?"

"Will anything I say go back to the police? You're not the police, right?"

"We are not the police, and if you want our conversation to remain between the three of us, then we can do that."

She looked unconvinced.

"And if you're afraid of something or someone, we can protect you, but only if tell us who or what that is."

Staring at the floor, she said, "Okay."

Vincent and I exchanged glances. "I promise we won't let them get to you."

With tears welling up, she said, "It's so bad. I don't even know where to start."

The fact she seemed remorseful made me think she wasn't the hardened criminal Ashworth painted her to be. "From the beginning. When you met Atlas to right now."

"Atlas came into the coffee shop I worked at. It was the first time I had ever seen him. He asked me out. And it was really great. After about a week, he told me loved me, and I told him the same. It felt so right. I'd never felt like that before."

"So, the relationship was good? He was nice to you?"

A single tear escaped, and she wiped it away. "Yeah, he called and texted all day long. He said he missed me and hated being away from me. Wanted to be with me twenty-four seven. It was sweet. I felt so special. He was like that for the whole three months before I moved in with him."

Love bombing.

"How did you end up in Jenner?"

"Atlas knew things weren't great at home, and I wanted to live a peaceful life. My father was awful. He had to control everything. By any means necessary. He'd berate my mother and hit her and me if we didn't do what he wanted or didn't live up to his expectations. He's awful. I still can't believe he agreed to look for me." She paused. "After a particularly bad episode with my dad, Atlas invited me to live with him on his farm. Thrilled, I agreed, and I told my mom where I was going, and I told Daphne. So, I packed up and left with Atlas. We drove up the coast to Jenner, to the community that you two came and visited. It was just like Atlas told you, living off the land. We all worked together to make dinners, to build a life."

She knew we had gone to the compound, and we were looking for her. Interesting. "Why didn't you call home to let people know you were in Jenner and you were safe?"

"When we arrived in Jenner, Atlas said in order to be part of the community, I had to get rid of everything from my old life —my cell phone, my names, my identity, and my relationships.

He took my cell phone, and he had me change my name to Fern."

Isolation.

"Were you free to roam around the community by yourself?"

"At first, we just stayed near the garden and in our cabin."

Mind swirling, I said, "Did Atlas ever let you go anywhere by yourself? Or have relationships or friendships without him?"

"I never went anywhere without him. I wasn't allowed to leave the community without him knowing about it."

"What about your clothes? Were you allowed to wear your old clothes?"

"No, because they were part of my old life. He said we all had to wear the same thing—clothes from the earth—linen, cotton. So, that's what we wore."

Controlling all aspects of her life.

"And everything was wonderful? You were happy?"

"At first, yeah. I loved the community, planting vegetables and harvesting them for our meals. It was so peaceful, like magical."

"When did that change?"

She let out a breath. "The first time I got upset with him was when I found him having relations with another woman in our community. But he told me I shouldn't worry about it, and it was okay because he believed in free love, and he was just sharing his love with other people. And there's nothing wrong with that."

"And you were okay with it?"

"No. And when I asked him if it was okay for me to share my love with other people, he said absolutely not because I was special and could only share my gift with him."

"He cheated on you just the one time?" My guess was *no way.*

Her head moved from side to side, indicating it wasn't only the one time. "He cheated all the time. And when I finally got fed up, he told me I was crazy, that I was overreacting, that this was a good thing. He was sharing his physical love, but he belonged to me."

Gaslighting.

"And what happened when you argued with him the last time?"

"He told me if I brought it up again, he would send me away."

Classic. "So you learned to be okay with him having physical relationships with other women?"

"I tried to be. But then one day, one woman he was sleeping with said that she was pregnant, and she was really upset. He told her she couldn't keep the baby. When she refused an abortion, he screamed at her and said, 'You will obey me.' And then he hit her so hard across the face that she fell to the ground. And that was the first time I thought maybe Atlas wasn't who I thought he was."

Intimidation.

"And then what happened?" I probed gently.

"After he hit the woman, he stormed off. I followed him and told him I would take the woman for an abortion. He said he appreciated that, but he would have someone else take care of her." With regret in her eyes, she said, "I don't know what happened to her. I never saw her again."

We sat quietly, waiting for her to continue.

"The next day, Atlas said he had a special job for me. I guess I'd passed his test. He told me his truth, that he was funding the community with drug money and wanted me to be part of the drug organization. Shocked, I asked how that fit with the community, and he said it was a necessary evil to keep our lifestyle and that it was all for the greater good."

"And you helped the organization?"

"Yes. He had me smuggle drugs from Southern California to the Bay Area. He said they could disguise me, that it would be easy. All I would have to do was drive down with him and pick up the product. The pickups only lasted until they rented the warehouse and found a new way to distribute the drugs. He said nobody would ever suspect a thing. And nobody ever did."

She looked down and cried.

I glanced over at Vincent, who grabbed tissues from the corner and brought them over to her. She accepted them, wiped her eyes, and continued her story. "The Brothers. That's what they called themselves. Atlas said they were trying to create a more enlightened society by distributing LSD. He said when you're under the influence of LSD, you can actually see God. Of course, he had me try it. I didn't see God, but I told him I had. So stupid."

"Did you handle the money for the drug organization?" I asked.

"No. I was never allowed any money. When I asked about that, he said he took care of everything, so I didn't need any money. In the community, we didn't use money."

"So, your role was to pick up the drugs from Southern California and bring them to the Bay Area."

"Yes."

"For how long?"

"For about a year."

"And things were going well? You were okay with that?"

She looked me dead in the eyes and said, "I believed it was for the greater good, for all of us, for mankind. But then, when he asked me..."

"He asked you what?" I urged.

"There was someone who wanted to jeopardize our way of life, to go to the police about the drugs. Her name was Opal. She wanted to expose us. She said what we were doing was wrong, that we were common drug dealers."

"And what happened to Opal?"

"Atlas said I had to take care of her. I had to gain her trust again so I could lure her in and kill her."

That must be the murder the DEA's confidential informant had mentioned.

With haunted eyes, she stared at Vincent and me. "And I can't stop thinking about it, her face, her body lying in that grave. I don't think I can ever erase it from my mind."

"I can imagine that would be difficult," I offered sympathetically.

"That's when I realized I needed to get away from him and that I couldn't live like that anymore. Looking back, I mean, it all seems so obvious. I was so stupid. How I fell for everything he said to me. But I did it. I killed her, and I tried to cope, but I couldn't hide how upset I was. I wasn't callous like him, so he kept me locked in our cabin. He told me I couldn't leave." She broke down and cried again.

Imprisonment, control.

All the classic signs of abuse were there. And so painfully clear to the informed outside observer. Love bombing, the first of the manipulation tactics, to make Katie feel loved and dependent on his affection in order to gain control. And then isolating her by taking her away from friends and family and telling her she couldn't communicate with them. Controlling all aspects of her life, from identity to communication to clothing to diet to movement. Gaslighting her, telling her she was overreacting to him sleeping around. Intimidation by harming others in front of her and then threatening to send her away. Making her dependent on him by not providing any financial means so she couldn't leave, and when she tried to, he imprisoned her.

"How did you escape?" I asked.

"I didn't. Well, I tried, and Atlas was upset. He moved me. I don't know where we were. He drove me somewhere, and these other men, they took me, and they kept me in a dark room."

"At the warehouse?" I guessed.

Her brows raised. "Yeah, at the warehouse."

"Continue."

"Then he moved me out of the warehouse and took me to a motel. He told me we were going to Mexico to lie low. We were waiting for our new identities. He said he knew how to disappear and that nobody would ever find us, and we would finally be happy and free."

"But you didn't believe him?" I asked.

"No. I pretended, but I didn't believe him. I came up with a plan to cause a car accident where he would be incapacitated, and I could get away. That happened on Friday night. I saw my opportunity, and I jumped out of the car before it hit a pole. I ran back in to get his cell phone so I could call for help and decided the only one likely to help was Daphne. She picked me up and took care of me. But then, the Brothers came after me, saying I took some of their drugs. I honestly don't know what they're talking about."

Listening to her, I could see she was torn up about the activities she had partaken in over the last two years. Her life had been a living hell, and she was trying to escape, or so it seemed.

After a quick glance at Vincent, I turned back to Katie. "Have you ever heard of the term 'coercive control'?"

She cocked her head. "No."

"It's a form of domestic violence. Abusers use patterns of behavior to control their victims. My firm specializes in helping survivors get out of dangerous situations safely. What you're describing sounds like a textbook case of coercive control. You weren't stupid. You were being manipulated, controlled, and being put into a position where you became desperate."

"But he... he... he never hit me."

"Coercive control doesn't work like that. Were you afraid of him?"

"Yes, I'd seen what he had done."

"Exactly, that's how it works. He had you scared for your life because you saw what he did to others. I can't tell you how to live your life, Katie, and we both agreed this would stay between the three of us, but I think we can help you. I think you should tell your story to the police."

"I'll go to jail, won't I?"

"It depends. How involved were you with the drug smuggling business? Do you know details? Do you remember faces, names, dates? Would you cooperate with the police if there was a case against the drug dealers?"

"Atlas told me a lot about the Brothers, and I met them several times."

Considering what she told me, I didn't question whether or not we could get her a deal. She had saved my life, and the crimes she committed were because of Atlas's manipulation, and it sounded like she acted under fear for her own life. Atlas was the bad guy here, not Katie. At least not totally. If I ran the world, I'd send Katie to a mental facility for intensive therapy to help her cope with the events of the last two years and growing up in an abusive home. She didn't belong in prison. And from the sounds of things, she may have enough information to take down the entire Brothers organization, which would be pretty valuable to the DEA.

"I'm going to talk to Sergeant Hirsch and see if there's anything he can do to help you. I won't tell him what you told us, just my gut feeling about how this could go. Do you think you would speak with them if we could get you a deal and ensure your safety?"

"I guess. If the police don't get me, the Brothers will."

"I'm going to talk to Hirsch and see what they can do, okay? Hang in there. Do you want me to call your parents?"

"I don't really want to see my dad, but my mom..."

She looked like a frightened child. I said, "I'll call your mom. Hang in there. This will work out."

"But I don't know if I deserve that."

"In my experience, sometimes things work out exactly how they need to, and how they should."

Unsure if she believed me, I exited with Vincent and met up with Hirsch in the conference room where the DEA agents, as well as Jayda and Ross, were waiting to hear about the interview.

"Did she tell you anything?" Hirsch asked.

Vincent replied, "She told us everything."

"Really?" Hirsch asked, surprised.

"Yes. If she talks, agrees to testify, can you make a deal for her?" I asked Agent Bishop.

Agent Bishop said, "If she's got information that could put Kenneth Martin and Jacob Briggs in jail forever, as well as her buddy Ryan Harris, I think we could make her a deal."

"She says if law enforcement doesn't get her, the Brothers will."

Agent Bishop said, "I don't doubt that."

"If we make a deal with her, we'll have to figure out a way to keep her safe."

Part of me thought I should go in with the DEA, so she wasn't alone. Agent Bishop could be intimidating to someone in Katie's position. I said, "Please go gentle. She's pretty broken up about everything that's happened, not just last night but for the last two years. She's likely a victim of intimate partner violence —coercive control. He never physically hurt her, other than detaining her and keeping her prisoner, but she is a victim, whether she understands it or not."

DEA Agent Bishop said, "Understood. We'll keep that in mind."

Hirsch stepped up to me. "Does she know a lot?"

"Sounds like she knows everything. You gotta get her a good deal, Hirsch. She's a victim."

With a brow raised, he said, "Did she really kill someone?"

Whatever I said would be hearsay. I nodded. "But it sounded like that was her breaking point. She couldn't handle it. She's remorseful, to say the very least."

"Good. If we can get her to talk, maybe we can hold these other guys accountable for the five Sunny D deaths, not to mention however many more we don't know about yet."

Fingers crossed.

47

―――――

FERN

Deep inside, I knew this was turning out too favorably for me. Why did I get options? A part of me believed I should be rotting in a prison—it was what I deserved. I had done terrible things, and even though Ms. Monroe insisted I was being forced and it wasn't entirely my fault, the guilt remained. I still couldn't unsee Opal's eyes, her body. It would haunt me for the rest of my life, that much I knew.

After speaking with agents from the DEA and the sheriff's department, I felt drained of every bit of energy. I was deflated, wanting to sleep for the rest of my life. But the sergeant had told me my mom was in the waiting room and eager to see me. Would she still love me if she knew what I had done?

The DEA insisted the only way I would be safe was if they put me in witness protection. However, they would only provide that if I agreed to testify in court against the Brothers— Kenneth Martin, Jacob Briggs, and Atlas, whose real name I had only just learned. When they revealed Atlas wasn't who he claimed to be, I wasn't entirely surprised, but I was shocked to learn he had been on the run from international law enforcement for the past ten years. Everything he had told me about his childhood, where he grew up, and his parents were all lies.

There was a time when I thought Atlas was my soulmate, but I never truly knew him. All I knew was a man who wanted to control everyone around him and make heaps of money selling drugs. I wondered how many other women he had duped. The agent had assured me I likely wasn't the first and that Atlas was a master manipulator. He would spend the rest of his life in jail once he recovered from the accident.

The past two years seemed unreal, much of it a facade meticulously crafted by Atlas. I had once believed he was the love of my life, but he was nothing more than a lying thief and drug dealer. If what they told me was true, it made sense to testify against him. They assured me they could protect me, that in a court of law, there were no weapons, except those held by law enforcement. Yet, I still feared standing on the witness stand, divulging everything I knew, especially knowing the people in the courtroom wanted me dead. I knew Atlas would kill me if he had the opportunity, especially after the car crash.

As I chewed on my fingernails, a childhood habit, I pondered my dilemma. If I didn't testify, I would go to prison, where the Brothers would likely find me, and I would die. My inner struggle wasn't about wanting to be free, starting over with a new identity. Rather, I contemplated whether I deserved to die, meeting the same fate as that woman whose real name I didn't even know.

Could I ever stop hating myself for participating in all those horrific acts, turning myself into a monster for a man?

My thoughts were interrupted as the door to the room opened. Our eyes met, and I stood up, never having felt more relieved or happy to see another person in my life—my mom. She had tears in her eyes, and she had aged more than the two years that had gone by since I'd seen her. She wrapped her arms around me, and we cried for a moment before she took a seat in the chair in front of me, and I followed suit.

"So good to see you," she whispered.

"You too. I'm so sorry. I'm so sorry for leaving, for not coming back. I'm so sorry for everything. I've done so many bad things," I cried.

"I love you. I'm just glad you're okay."

She probably couldn't fathom what I had done.

"The police say they're holding you. They wouldn't tell me why. They said I should talk to you."

They were going to make me speak my truth to my mother, forcing me to face the music on my own. I got myself into this mess; it was my responsibility. I wasn't a child anymore, and I had to be truthful. "I've done some bad things, and they aren't going to let me go unless..."

"Unless what?"

"Unless I testify in court against some really terrible people."

"How bad? I don't understand. Where have you been? I just... I don't understand any of it."

This was the woman who gave me life; she deserved to know. "Like I told you, I was moving with Atlas to be with him on his farm..." I told her everything that had happened, what I had told the DEA, and what they were asking in return for my freedom, for a new identity, for a new life. I had to leave everything behind if I were to go that route. After I explained to them why I had run away in the first place, they told me if I wanted to take my mom with me, she could go too, if she wanted to.

My heart broke as I watched my mother cry, unable to speak after hearing the atrocities I'd committed. I didn't blame her. I felt the same way—broken, torn up, never to be put back together again.

"I'm so sorry, Mom. I'm sorry for all of it."

After she calmed herself, and having gone through half of the box of tissue, she finally said, "If you testify against these people, you'll be safe."

"I will, but I can never come back to the Bay Area. I can never talk to anybody from my old life, ever again."

The irony wasn't lost on me. The path I had chosen would lead me to this point. With Atlas, I thought I was starting a new life, a good one, but it was misguided. Now I would have to start over again, but this time it was to save my life.

"What are you going to do?" she asked.

"I don't know. I'm really scared."

With determination, she said, "Testify."

"The DEA and the district attorney said you could come with me. New identity. Dad would never ever hurt you ever again. He won't find us."

She whispered, "This is all my fault. If I had left him, if I hadn't made you be in that house with him, this never would've happened. I'm so sorry, baby girl. I'm so sorry."

"This is not your fault, Mom. It's my fault."

"No, it's not. I should've left him years ago. I didn't have the strength. I'm so sorry."

We had never spoken about my father's abuse. It was an unspoken horror that we lived daily; my mom got the worst of it. "I don't think that's true, Mom. The PI you hired said it's very hard to leave, to get out. She specializes in helping people get to safety. You can't beat yourself up, Mom. He spent enough years doing that."

With dry eyes, my mother looked at me and said, "I'll do it."

"You'll go with me into witness protection?"

"If you testify, I'll go with you. It's time we break the cycle. You and me."

Ms. Monroe had explained my home life had made it seem

like the things Atlas had done to me were normal. Despite thinking I had run away from a controlling, abusive man, I had run straight into the arms of someone just like him, but Atlas was even worse.

48

HIRSCH

Inside the Sunny D task force room, formerly called the Cold Case Squad room, I knew this was the last meeting, at least for a while. The team, including the DEA agents in charge of the Brothers' organization task force, sat around the table, ready to provide the latest update. It had been several days since we arrested Kenneth Martin and Jacob Briggs and Peña had lost his life. Atlas was still in the hospital, but there were plans for his incarceration once he was fit enough to be moved.

Agent Bishop of the DEA stood next to the projector screen and said, "First off, I'd like to thank everybody in this room. Not only have you helped us solve one of the biggest cases the DEA has taken on, as well as your own, but you've done it with the utmost professionalism and openness. You kept it quiet, no leaks. That's pretty rare."

With confidence, I said, "Well, if our paths cross again, you'll know you can trust us."

"Absolutely. I am blown away by this team's effort, and upon getting to know some of you a little better, it's not a surprise that tough cases are your specialty. And now I know if we work together again, we'll be successful." A rare smile appeared on Bishop's face, and he continued. "My superiors want to thank you and let you know we're always looking for fresh talent at the DEA. Hint, hint."

Not a chance, but it was a nice gesture.

The sheriff sat up straight and said, "I'd like to echo that sentiment. I know this team, and I promise you, as long as we have the budget available, we will reach out for your help. I'm looking at you, Martina and Vincent."

Martina smiled and said, "Drakos Monroe Security & Investigations would appreciate the business. We would be more than happy to come back, given the right circumstances."

My emotions were all over the place. Thrilled we closed the case that had nearly gotten Martina killed. Not to mention, the five who died from overdoses and the six additional bodies discovered when they raided the Jenner property, including the woman Katie had referred to as Opal.

But I felt melancholy too. The case was closed which meant my rear was back behind the desk with Martina and Vincent back at their firm. Looking out at our team, I said, "Thank you all. This team is always a pleasure to work with, and I appreciate your consistency, your friendship, and your camaraderie." Shifting my gaze to Agent Bishop and his crew, I said, "And to our new colleagues from the DEA. We love to cross jurisdictions and step in all kinds of things. This isn't likely to be the last you'll hear from us." Chuckling sounded. "My gratitude to you and the team for working with a shared vision. Now, I'm dying to know what your team has found and what's going to happen to the Brothers."

"Thanks, Hirsch. Without further ado," Agent Bishop continued. "As all of you know, the DEA raided the property in Jenner and the warehouse in Santa Rosa. After the statements from Katie Kimble, we searched Atlas's blue SUV from the car wreck. Sure enough, we found boxes of bars of soap with tablets of LSD laced with fentanyl inside. The discovery explains why the Brothers went after Atlas and Katie. Not only that, but with the seizure, we linked it to the five deaths you were investigating. Based on this discovery, we can charge Ryan Harris, Kenneth Martin, and Jacob Briggs with five counts of murder. Ryan Harris is looking at an additional six for the bodies found on the Jenner property and charges from Scotland Yard he had evaded more than a decade ago. Kenneth Martin and Jacob Briggs will have additional charges for attempted murder, unlawful detainment, and distribution of a controlled substance from the night you brought them in. Our team has also arrested an additional twenty-seven members of the Brothers' organization down in Southern California. With the evidence collected, and Katie's agreement to testify in open court, we suspect the case should go off without a hitch and their prosecution solidified."

Martina said, "Katie and her mom are going into witness protection?"

"Yes, we've been in constant contact with Katie, and she's agreed to testify. She and her mother will go into witness protection in exchange for Katie's testimony, which is pivotal for putting these guys away for life."

Martina's face brightened, and I could tell that made her happy. As a father, I understood the need to want the best for your child, to want them to be happy and healthy. But as I'd seen with Kim and Martina and Mrs. Kimble, there was something about a mother's bond that no man, no force, no law could break or get between.

"What about our low-level dealers?" I asked.

"We're still rounding up quite a few, but for the two you have in custody, Ashworth Dante and Zander Jenkins, we want to talk about charges. Ashworth is refusing to testify, but we'd like to propose probation; he has no priors. We think this might've scared him straight. Zander's a kid with a record."

"But he's a good kid underneath it. I can tell. If he's given a chance…"

Agent Bishop gave a knowing nod. "We saw your statement from the initial interview. And we understand you've been in contact with social services, trying to get him clean?"

"Yes, social services should be here today." I only hoped Zander took the lifeline we were offering him.

"We agree probation is adequate, with stipulations of course. One is that he continues in school and keeps straight during his four years of probation. Is that acceptable?"

Relieved, I said, "Yes."

At least something good could come out of this case. Maybe one kid never given a chance would get one. Sometimes the strangest circumstances can bring about the best-case scenario.

I didn't know if it was my age or my status as a parent, but looking back over my life, I could clearly connect all the dots that led me to where I was. Some things I would've never thought could put me on the path to a life I loved and cherished, in fact, had. Like a wife and a daughter who were my whole world, and they wouldn't be, if all those dots hadn't connected.

I hoped to be one of those dots in Zander's life.

"Any questions?"

"When do you think it will go to court?" I asked.

"We think this is going to cause a ruckus in the press. The DEA will make a formal statement at the end of the day, releasing the identities of the top three suspects. We will keep the low-level guys out of the press considering they're not going into WITSEC. We don't want the rest of the Brothers or any spinoffs going after them. But we will parade Ken Martin, Jacob Briggs, and Ryan Harris on the news. They'll be the poster boys for what happens when you think you can drug and kill innocent people. But the actual trial will likely take months to years to get in front of a jury."

At the end of the meeting, there were cheers and job-well-dones from nearly everyone in the room.

When the room quieted down to just a few, Martina approached and sat next to me. "How do you feel, boss?"

"Like I'm ready for a nap."

"Or a vacation?"

"Something like that."

"You know, this is definitely one of the tougher cases solved by a team of private investigators, the sheriff's department detectives, and the DEA. It's pretty special, Hirsch."

It was, but it wasn't over until the bars on their cells shut for good. "I agree."

"Are you worried they won't get convicted?"

"Until it actually goes to trial and I hear the sentences, it won't be closed in my mind. A lot can happen between now and then."

I had seen solid cases fall apart. Hopefully, they had Katie and her mother secure, where nobody could silence them. If the Brothers got to them, I doubted the case would move forward how the DEA wanted it to.

"Take the win, Hirsch. We'll celebrate with a barbecue at my house."

"We'll be there."

My sadness and apprehension weren't just my fear the Brothers wouldn't get life in prison. It was also another ending, a glimpse of what used to be and it ending again. Martina didn't seem as down. Maybe it was her woman's intuition, telling her this wasn't the last of our partnership. It was just one more dot that would lead us to where we were intended to be all along.

49

MARTINA

THE SUN WAS SHINING, with just a spattering of clouds in the baby blue sky as a mix of the old Cold Case Squad and the Sunny D task force were happily munching on burgers and hotdogs. Fingertips touched mine, and Wilder squeezed my hand. "Looks like you're deep in thought."

"Just grateful for all my blessings," I replied. One of those blessings was Wilder. I'd kept my promise, and after the case was closed and Katie was safely in law enforcement's custody, we went out again. And again. And again.

The situation, Wilder sitting in my back yard, holding my hand as I looked out at my family, both chosen and blood, wasn't one I could have imagined. I thanked the Lord for all my blessings, but I knew everything could change in a heartbeat. But I was working on being grateful for what I had in the moment and not worrying about what could happen in the future. Things were good, and I was happy. I said, "So, you've met everyone now?"

"Yes, and they all say you're the toughest woman they know, but they're also fiercely protective of you. I have to watch my back for sure."

"I would love to say their bark is louder than their bite." I chuckled. "But it's not."

Zoey walked up to us. It felt a little strange, my hand entwined with Wilder's in front of my daughter. She barely remembered Jared, but it seemed wrong, yet she was fully team "Wildtina." Apparently, that was our names mashed together. "Hey, Mom. Hi, Wilder. Vincent and Amanda just arrived. You ought to go say hello," she said with an exaggerated, "hello."

Studying my daughter, I could see she knew something—a secret. "What's up?"

"You'll just have to go say hi to find out."

Audrey rolled up and clasped her arms around Zoey's waist. Zoey looked down. "Hi, Audrey."

"Hi, Zoey. Want to play with me and Barney?"

"Of course." Zoey looked back at me, and I was reminded of what a lovely young woman she had become. And how fortunate and thankful I was that she was safe and sound and right there with me. "Vincent and Amanda are at the cupcake table looking very cozy, but I'm sure they'd love to see you." She giggled and ran off with Audrey.

I cocked my head, intrigued by some secret knowledge my daughter seemed to have about Vincent and Amanda. I said, "Time to learn what all the fuss is about," and lifted myself up and out of the grasp of Wilder's warm hand as I set off to the dessert table filled with cupcakes. My daughter and mother had baked lemon chiffon and chocolate with peanut butter frosting. I had eaten one of each and prayed I didn't fall into a sugar coma.

"Hey, Vincent. Hi, Amanda. How have you been?"

She wrapped her arm around Vincent's shoulder and wiggled her fingers. Adorning her left ring finger was a sparkling diamond and on her face, a dazzling smile.

"Is this what I think it is?" I asked, playing coy.

Amanda squealed. "He just proposed! We're getting married."

My heart was full. "Congratulations to both of you!" Vincent and I embraced, and then I hugged Amanda. "I'm so happy for the two of you."

Amanda said, "I was told that perhaps you nudged Vincent along."

"My only advice was to be a better communicator, that's all. Everything else was all Vincent."

She stared at her finger, admiring her new engagement ring, and said, "I suppose he's a keeper."

"Hey," Vincent playfully interjected. They shared a brief kiss, and he whispered, "I love you, Amanda."

"I love you, Vincent."

It seemed fitting that we were next to a table full of sugar; perhaps the sweetness was contagious.

Ross chimed in, "Get a room, you two." He laughed and said, "Congratulations, Vincent and Amanda. Although, Amanda, you could do better. If you're looking, I can hook you up."

Vincent acted offended. "Hey."

"Only joking. He's a good one, Amanda."

"I know," she said giddily.

Hirsch approached and said, "What am I hearing? Squealing? What's going on?"

"Aren't you a detective?" I teased.

He glanced at Amanda and Vincent and said, "Congratulations to the both of you."

"Thank you, August."

"Thanks, Sarge."

And like that, we had a team who not only excelled at bringing justice but also were thriving in relationships. There was something special that bonded us all together. Whether it was God or some sort of universal magic, I didn't know, but I was grateful. As much as I didn't wish for crime to continue, I couldn't wait for the next big case where we had the opportunity to work together again. Hirsch and I exchanged a knowing smile. I wasn't a betting woman, but if I were, I'd be inclined to guess Hirsch was thinking the exact same thing.

THANK YOU!

Thank you for reading *Who She Was*! I hope you enjoyed reading it as much as I loved writing it. If you did, I would greatly appreciate if you could post a short review.

Reviews are crucial for any author and can make a huge difference in visibility of current and future works. Reviews allow us to continue doing what we love, *writing stories*. Not to mention, I would be forever grateful!

Thank you!

ACKNOWLEDGMENTS

Like most of my stories, I gather inspiration from non-fiction and true crime sources such as books, documentaries, and podcasts. This one's no different!

One afternoon I was listening to the Wine & Crime Podcast where they were describing the Brotherhood of Eternal Love and I thought it was totally bonkers. I then listened to the audiobook *Orange Sunshine: The Brotherhood of Eternal Love and Its Quest to Spread Peace, Love, and Acid to the World* by Nicholas Schou and narrated by Stephen Bowlby. Fascinating! It definitely sparked my creativity to form a modern day commune with drug trafficking roots.

But, as the title *Who She Was* implies, the story is really about a woman manipulated into doing terrible things by her boyfriend using coercive control. I have done a lot of reading in this area because it's fascinating (and terrible). One book I read a few years back, that hit me hard and has stuck with me ever since I first read it was *No Visible Bruises: What We Don't Know About Domestic Violence Can Kill Us* by Rachel Louise Snyder. It's insightful and heartbreaking. I truly wish I could gift this book to every single person on the planet.

There are so many misconceptions about domestic (intimate partner) violence that it has inspired several of my stories, include my very first thriller *Not Like Her*, Selena Bailey Book 1 and Martina's role at her firm (helping survivors leave abusers safely) in an attempt to throw in a little education while entertaining.

In addition to the above inspirations, I want to extend many thanks to those who helped me shape and create this story.

First, thank you to my Advanced Reader Team. My ARC Team is invaluable in taking the first look at my stories and helping find typos and spreading awareness of my stories through their reviews and kind words.

Thank you to my editors, Paula Leste, Becky Stewart, and Ryan Mahan.

To my cover designer, Odile, thank you for your guidance and talent. You are incredible!

Last but not least, I'd like to thank all of my readers. It's because of you I'm able to continue writing stories.

ALSO BY H.K. CHRISTIE

The Martina Monroe Series —a nail-biting crime thriller series starring PI Martina Monroe and her unofficial partner Detective August Hirsch of the Cold Case Squad. If you like high-stakes games, jaw-dropping twists, and suspense that will keep you on the edge of your seat, then you'll love the Martina Monroe crime thriller series.

The Selena Bailey Series (1 - 5) — a suspenseful series featuring a young Selena Bailey and her turbulent path to becoming a top-notch private investigator as led by her mentor, Martina Monroe.

The Val Costa Series —a gripping crime thriller with heart-pounding suspense. If you love Martina, you'll love Val.

The Neighbor Two Doors Down —a dark and witty psychological thriller. If you like unpredictable twists, page-turning suspense, and unreliable narrators, then you'll love *The Neighbor Two Doors Down*.

A Permanent Mark A heartless killer. Weeks without answers. Can she move on when a murderer walks free? If you like riveting suspense and gripping mysteries then you'll love *A Permanent Mark* - starring a grown up Selena Bailey.

For H.K. Christie's full catalog go to: **www.authorhkchristie.com**

At **www.authorhkchristie.com** you can also sign up for the H.K. Christie reader club where you'll be the first to hear about upcoming novels, new releases, giveaways, promotions, and a free e-copy of the prequel to the Martina Monroe Thriller Series, *Crashing Down*!

ABOUT THE AUTHOR

H. K. Christie watched horror films far too early in life. Inspired by the likes of Stephen King, Dean Koontz, true crime podcasts, and a vivid imagination she now writes suspenseful thrillers.

She found her passion for writing when she embarked on a one-woman habit breaking experiment. Although she didn't break her habit she did discover a love of writing and has been at it ever since.

When not working on her latest novel, H.K. Christie can be found eating & drinking with friends, walking around the lakes, or playing with her favorite furry pal.

She is a native and current resident of the San Francisco Bay Area.

To learn more about H.K. Christie and her books, or simply to say, "hello", go to **www.authorhkchristie.com**.

At **www.authorhkchristie.com** you can also sign up for the H.K. Christie reader club where you'll be the first to hear about upcoming novels, new releases, giveaways, promotions, and a free e-copy of the prequel to the Martina Monroe Thriller Series, *Crashing Down!*